BOBBY CARAPISI

(Volume II)

First Edition

Published by The Nazca Plains Corporation
Las Vegas, Nevada
2009

ISBN: 978-1-935509-55-4

Published by

The Nazca Plains Corporation ®
4640 Paradise Rd, Suite 141
Las Vegas NV 89109-8000

PUBLISHER'S NOTE
Bobby Carapisi is a work of fiction created wholly by *Kyle Michel
Sullivan*'s imagination. All characters are fictional and any resemblance
to any persons living or deceased is purely by accident. No portion of
this book reflects any real person or events.

Cover Photos
Mircea Bezergheanu and MaxFx

Art Director
Blake Stephens

DEDICATION

To the guys I know who've been through this.

BOBBY CARAPISI

(Volume II)

First Edition

A Novel By

Kyle Michel Sullivan

CONTENTS

"ERIC"

I hate getting calls on Wednesday nights. Somehow I'd got caught up in "Law & Order: SVU" and now I'm totally hot for Chris Meloni, even though he's darker and more "daddy" than I usually like. But I was out of crystal. And low on vodka. And watching "Elliot" go through his butch-buff dance with "Olivia" was going to get me in the mood, anyway, so I answered it.

He told me his name was Harris, he's in town for business and wanted "some company" at eleven. Was I available then? It was just past ten. Not much time but do-able, so I said, sure, and took down his info. He was at a hotel on Santa Monica ("motel", it sounded like). Which was zero surprise; they're always at some low-rent roach trap when they call off of this particular ad; I have four (with photo) going in the back of the semi-weeklies. I snagged a quickie shower, neatened the three-day growth on my latest goatee, slipped into my tight black jeans and tee shirt and wriggled my ass straight over.

It was a nicer place than I expected; new concrete and black glass, trendy shops just closing up, ten dollar coffee joints packed with loud happy queens. I grabbed a parking spot just before some character trying to make a "U-turn" could get it. He cursed and spit, but I shrugged him off. LA drivers are such assholes, me included.

I always make it a point to arrive a few minutes early, partly so I can make sure nobody who looks like a vice cop is lounging around and partly to knock on the door at the exact moment I'm due. This habit of being punctual was drilled into me by my Dad, who on more than one occasion either left me standing outside a movie theater, or refused to accompany me someplace, or just plain would not let Mom serve me dinner because I dared to be a few minutes late. It was drilled into him by Gramma, (who for all her Minnesota sweetness could still be as harsh as our Georgia Grandmother). I still get tense when I even THINK I'm running a minute behind. So there I was, looking sleek and sexy, standing before room 204 at eleven p.m. sharp (I heard a newscast starting in some room down the hall).

I hit the buzzer and the door opened. A middle-aged man in a sharp business suit, his hair salt and pepper, his smile wide and natural, his eyes hard as diamonds, stood there, a drink in one hand, the door handle in the other.

"Harris?" I asked. "I'm Joshua."

He looked me over, and I flashed back to a PBS special about leopards and their prey. It was made up of your usual pretty shots of big bad kitty cats prowling through the brush. Until this one moment. Where a leopard lying in wait noticed a gazelle fawn wandering too far from its mother. Its eyes locked on the little critter. Its movements froze. Every muscle in its body sharpened in anticipation of attack. Then it snapped in for an instant kill. That was "Harris", pure jungle instinct wrapped in a thousand dollar suit and way-too-perfect grooming.

Still to all intents and purposes, he would have seemed to be exactly what I should expect. Except his tie was still tight around his neck. And his jaw tensed in triumph when he saw me. And his smile threatened to widen. And this little robot in my head started screeching, "Danger, Eric Larson! Danger, danger!" I hesitated, weighing whether or not to even enter the room. I mean, did I REALLY want to find out what this guy's dreams were, let alone fulfill them?

But then he answered, "Yes, I'm Harris. Come in."

He stepped back, indicating I should enter. So I did. You see, I may not have been at this for all that long, but I knew the drill; I got tips from some of the more experienced guys I'd come to know. If I back out now and this guy's a cop, he'll know I "made" him. Then I'll keep getting calls from other entrapment fucks till I mess one up and wind up in county for however long. And if I run, he can bust me for resisting arrest. No, all I had to do was keep from doing anything that proved I intended to follow through with whatever proposition he offered, to keep myself safe. And if he was just a sadistic creep? Well, I did have my hockey skills to fall back on – which I DID fall back on, not so long ago, with a drunk who thought two-hundred bucks bought him access to anything he damn well wanted, and who the fuck was I to say no.

It was a decent room – one big bed extending from a wall, TV on the dresser against the opposite wall, chairs and table by the window, curtains drawn to keep it private, all so new and SO tacky. But I'd seen so many of them over the past five – no, four months, I didn't even care to notice how bad the color scheme was. What I did notice was a woman seated at the table, a PowerBook open and ready in front of her; and that WAS highly unusual.

I turned to him and said, "Your name's not Harris."

"Any more than yours is Joshua, Mr. Larson." He closed the door and sat on the edge of the dresser, the ice clinking in his drink. "I'm Wilson Lewis. This is my associate, Ms. Calvert. You're a difficult young man to get hold of."

"Yeah, right," I snapped. "And the clichéd response for that comment is, 'Not difficult enough'."

I'd been getting messages from this creep for the past three weeks, identifying himself as an attorney representing "Mr. William Allen Barrow" and first asking, then insisting, then demanding I call him back to discuss "matters of very grave importance." Like there was any way in hell I wanted to discuss anything with that motherfucker or his lawyer. I'd kept ignoring them, hoping he'd catch the hint and dissolve into nothingness; obviously, that was a fool's dream.

"I apologize for the subterfuge," he smiled, "but we very much need to speak with you. And if that means scheduling a meeting into your normal 'business' routine, so be it."

"Golly, you mean you don't want to suck me off?" I asked. Ms. Calvert blinked in shock. Obviously she was not used to such raw language coming from so tender a creature as myself. I think I smirked as I thought that thought.

Lewis handled it better. His smile widened as he said, "That holds no interest for me."

I shrugged and headed for the door. He rose. I just glided around him, hands up and visible for Ms. Calvert to see. No way was I going to give him a chance to slap me with assault charges.

"Eric, please, just listen, will you?" he said. I opened the door. "Eric, this is childish! Don't force me to file charges against you."

I stopped. And I looked at him. "For what?"

"Filing a false police report."

I knew instantly what he was referring to, but I had zero intention of making it easy for him. "And just when the fuck did I do that?"

"You filed assault charges against my client. We want them withdrawn."

"The DA dropped them."

"The assistant district attorney refused to follow through with the charges, yes. To completely clear the slate, the complainant must officially request the charges be dropped."

So that WAS it. Allen was using this four-bit pit-bull to clean up his "good name." Well, the hell with that. I left the door open and stormed over to Lewis, my temper flaring.

"Your fucking client kidnapped and raped me! In my mouth! And up my ass! And anywhere else he fucking could! Along with two of his fucking friends! So you tell Mr. William Allen Fucking Barrow to go fuck himself! You'll see fucking snow cones in hell before I do one fucking thing for him!"

Wouldn't you know it? Nobody came down the hall or peeked in the door. It was like the "Hotel California", or something; all deserted or

4

deliberate deafness. Ignore the screaming; just a bit of business being transacted; happens all the time.

Lewis calmly strolled over and closed the door. Then he turned on me. And those diamond sharp eyes of his sliced right through me.

"Drop the charges, Eric, or I'll put you in jail. And you'd better believe I can."

Looking back, I now realize that was when I should have just walked. I might have wound up arrested and maybe even spent a few days in the Twin Towers (LA County Jail), but that would've been nothing compared to what happened. Instead, I got more pissed. That happens to me, sometimes; I just plain get to a point where I say, "Fuck it", and plow headlong into whatever it is trying to beat me down or hold me back or make me change. And what little common sense I have goes into the trash. It's nowhere near heroic; it's just stupidly stubborn. But never let it be said that I backed down in the face of my own annihilation. I went nose to nose with him, so close I could smell the bourbon on his breath.

"You want a swearing match?" I snarled. "Fine. Let's have at it! You think because he's had the same job for twenty years and owns a house and has lots and lots of friends to vouch for his character, that all the judge'll see in me is a fucked-up male whore who tried to hustle him?! You think I haven't already been through this shit with that cunt of a DA?! With every lawyer I've talked to about suing him? 'It's your word against his, Eric, and that's not enough.' So do it! Drag me into court! Try and throw the fuckin' book at me! 'Cause with all the words and other bullshit aside, it's also just his word against mine!"

"Eric, Mr. Barrow's told his employer he's homosexual. It didn't matter. He's a good employee; they want to keep him."

Danger! Danger! But did I listen? "What the fuck's that got to do with anything?!"

"It means we can use the video. We can show it to the judge. Make it more than his word against yours."

And then WHOOSH! BAM! SMASH! That word finally hit me – "video." He kept talking, but it's like that one word shut down every synapse in my brain's hearing region to give me a moment to process this new explosion of information.

Video. We can use the video. Show it to the judge. A video. Make it more than just his word against yours. With a Video. A video! A fucking VIDEO!

The words pinged about in my little pinball brain, dinging here and beeping there and not doing a damned thing to make any of it any clearer. I finally backed away and motioned for him to stop talking. He did.

"You said 'video'," I whispered. "What do you mean?"

He rolled his eyes. "You know perfectly well."

"No, I don't. What do you mean? What video?"

"These games are getting us nowhere."

"What fucking video are you fucking talking about?!"

"The one you and he recorded! And signed a release for!"

He and I recorded? Allen and me? A video Allen made of our encounter? That he AND I shot? And I signed a release? I put my name on a piece of paper that said "okay" to that?

My knees turned to jelly and I flopped onto the bed. And I said in the most normal voice in the world, "But we didn't record anything."

Lewis sighed and lay his head in one hand, like he was at the end of his rope.

I kept talking. "No, no, there was no camera in that room. Believe me, I would have remembered. Every detail of that place is seared into my mind. The four walls. And no windows. Just bright light and the bed. And the chair. And-and-and there was no camera there!" Except that I was blindfolded through it all, even after I gave in and let them do as they wanted. So how would I know? How could I know? But that little detail didn't really come knocking at my brain till later.

"Eric, please, I have a copy of it."

My voice began to crack. "Bullshit! This isn't some fucked up game, you son-of-a-bitch, so quit fuckin' with me! What'd he do? He go out and find some guy that looks like me and shoot some hi-def and show you that? He'd better be my fuckin' twin right down to my fuckin' dick!"

He sighed, again, then picked up a remote and hit it. That's when I noticed the television was connected to a little portable DVD player.

Suddenly everything shifted into this staccato feeling. Me. My thoughts. My awareness. He was definitely going to show me something to back up his claim. And I wondered if I was about to be proven completely crackers.

The TV clicked on. And I appeared on camera. Naked. Tied. Spread-eagle on the bed. Face up. The gag pulled down around my neck. The blindfold still around my eyes. The image was from a three-quarter slightly overhead angle. And I was in perfect view. All of me. And Allen was working. On me. And boy, did he have me going. I didn't DO anything, just let him work me like a pro – but still – .

It reminded me of a bondage video Vic showed me, once. Some VHS piece of crap from New Jersey. With a "victim" who couldn't act strung up in some storage room and being "forced to enjoy" being given (then giving) a blowjob. It was so stupid and amateurish, I'd laughed my ass off all the way through it. But as I watched this one, my feet and hands went cold. And I felt like I was slipping out of reality.

I vaguely recognized this was from the middle of the ordeal. When my resistance was completely gone. Allen's hands were focused on my tits. With his mouth slamming away on my – on my dick. And I was squirming and giving off these little grunts that could have been pain or pleasure (or gas, for all you could really tell). I don't specifically remember him getting me to shoot, again, but I did remember staying hard. Viagra works, it seems, so long as there's external stimulation.

Then the angle changed. There was a "cut"! An edit! The camera moved to a side angle! And there I was. Lying back on the bed. In full glory. Being stroked. Till I ejaculated. Came. Shot. The whole fucking nine yards! Holy fucking shit, I was in a porno video. A fucking New Jersey bondage porno video.

No, no, no, what I was seeing could not be happening. It just couldn't be. No way. Allen and his buddies had fucking RECORDED it all? To watch over and over again as they jacked off? And to laugh about? And maybe SHARE, along with some choice stories, with other perverts like themselves?!

My stomach gave a jolt and my mouth began to water, and without even thinking I bolted for the bathroom. I barely made it in before I hurled my nuked dinner everywhere. Most of it hit the toilet, but not all. Not by a long shot. I heard Lewis behind me, asking, "Are you all right?" I kicked the door shut in his face. Then I hurled, again.

I don't know how long I kept going, but I was way into the dry heaves before I was able to regain control. Then I slid to the floor and sat there, shaking. Unable to think. Unable to believe what I'd just seen. I just kept hearing, "They recorded it. They fucking recorded it," in this never-ending loop that echoed in my brain.

Listen, I know I wasn't right with myself, back then. I wasn't healthy. Wasn't handling my trauma in a way that would heal me. But at least I'd bought into the idea that it WAS behind me. And I don't know, maybe I'd have pulled myself together, eventually. Seen the male-whore thing was not exactly laden with prospects. Hit the floor and bounced around then risen to stand on my own two feet, again. I remember somebody someplace (maybe it was Lucia) telling me it can take up to three years to get over an ordeal like this, and you have to find a way to deal with it till your mind and soul are as strong as your body, again.

But seeing that? It put me right back to one. "Okay folks, let's have another take. Try and get it right, this time." And it was like the last five months (no, it WAS just four months since that night) had been wiped away and I was back to the morning after, waiting on that gurney for my next trauma. Jesus Christ, could I go through that, again?

I didn't know.

I finally dragged myself to my feet and washed off as best I could. It didn't do much good; my t-shirt and jeans were flecked with the crap from my innards (as one southern relative called them, once), and sponging at it only seemed to make the mess worse. I gave up and looked in the mirror. The person looking back at me was like something out of "The Wax Museum." Glossy skin. Glassy eyes. Nylon hair. Coloring all wrong. None of it moved; none of it breathed; none of it looked right. It was just this lifeless shape propped against the sink on the other side of the mirror, set up to gaze back at whoever came to the counter. I could do nothing to make it any different.

I flushed the toilet, cleaned up the bathroom, washed my face and hands and popped in some "Dentyne" to chew. All good whores have some kind of breath crap; nothing like gingivitis to kill a tip. Then I straightened myself up and stepped out of the bathroom.

I leaned against the doorframe and stared at this stupid little pattern in the cheap wallpaper. It was like a "fleur de lis" but something was missing from it. Or the petals were short. Or there was too much to it. Something. It just didn't look right. Lewis came over to me.

"Eric?" he asked. "Are you feeling better?"

I refused to look at him; if I had, I'd have ripped his fucking throat out. I just said, "Where I come from, it's impolite to address someone by their Christian name without first asking their permission." Grandmother's Southern "fuck off" attitude seemed best, at that moment.

He waited a moment then said, "Aren't we beyond that?"

I just focused on that stupid pattern in the wallpaper that made no sense. Like everything else make no sense. Or too much. "That's why they left the blindfold on. That's what Chaps meant when he said, 'Yes, yes.' He got a good shot. Well-framed. Nice angle."

"You're still maintaining you knew nothing about the video?" Lewis asked in a disbelieving voice.

I jumped. I hadn't realized I was talking out loud. I still did not look at him. "I didn't."

"You were obviously involved in what Allen was doing with you."

"I wanted it over! By that point, I'd have done anything for it to be over!"

"Including maintain an erection? Including ejaculate?"

"Cut it out. They fed me Viagra and GHB. It's in the tox-report. And I didn't shoot, not during that part."

"That's not what it shows at the end."

"I only ejaculated earlier. After the one who looked like a wrestler. And Allen. Forced me to."

"Eric..."

I pushed past him and grabbed the remote. I paused the DVD. Saw it was at the point where I was face down (they'd let it run while I spewed my guts out? Assholes!) I clicked to go back at an 8x speed. Allen's and my movements jerked into hyper-speed, making the whole fucking thing look ludicrous. The angles changed back and forth between the overhead shot and a closer three-quarter side view. Aimed right at me. They zoomed in and out just like other videos do, but usually they were static.

Suddenly I was no longer spread-eagle; I was just lying on the bed and they were close on my – fuck it, on my dick. I was semi-hard and flopping on my groin. The camera zoomed back to show my feet were held apart by those cuffs. My pants and shirt pulled away to reveal me. My underwear gone. The next shot was of me half-stripped and bound and gagged in the back of the van, the camera playing over my body in close-up. Then came me walking backwards down Melrose in my black jeans and shirt.

I blinked. No proof of anything here except Allen gave me a blowjob then fucked me. All by himself. Alone. Even the zooms were simple enough to have been done by remote.

I fast-forwarded back to when I was first lying on the bed and hit the "play" button to watch it at regular speed. The shot began after I'd already had my briefs ripped way, but you could still see shreds of them peeking out from underneath me.

"This is from the beginning," I whispered. "From when this first started."

"In preparation to be engaged in Allen's little 'fantasy'."

"Go fuck yourself." I fast-forwarded to where it showed me ejaculating. Allen's mouth pulled back but his hand kept going. Until I shot (well, dribbled, actually) back over myself.

"This is from the same shot," I said. "You can tell the positioning is the same. It's wrong for when I'm tied. On the bed."

"Doesn't matter," said Lewis. "If I show this to the District Attorney, I'm fairly certain I could get charges presented against you."

I sighed. "Probably. Ionescue didn't even try to hide how homophobic she is. You get her, she'll pounce on this."

"Then you will officially withdraw the charges against my client?"

Suddenly, I was tired. Weary to the bone, as Gramma'd say. I hadn't noticed anything on that monitor to support my story – except what could be passed off as "continuity errors." Nice job of editing, motherfuckers. It was all I could do to shrug. "Why not? It's not like anything was gonna get done, anyway."

"Excellent," said Lewis. "And to think I thought YOU'D be unreasonable. Would you still like to be paid for your time?"

"You got what you wanted," I whispered. "You gotta twist the knife?"

I noticed I'd let the thing keep playing. I tried to hit "stop" but only hit "fast-forward" in 8x speed. It now showed jerky images of Allen helping me put on my shirt. Even that quick, it looked to me like I was in shock (which I was), but I could see Lewis arguing I was just stoned. Or filled with pleasure. A lot of people would at least wonder if he was right.

I finally stopped it, rose and headed for the door. I knew I was awake, but I couldn't convince myself of it. I wobbled like someone walking for the first time after a decade-long coma. I was thinking – nothing, really; I was too numb. Everything I was doing was by rote.

Until I reached the door.

The cold metal of the knob zapped me with a static shock and a phrase popped into my mind. "And to think I thought YOU'd be unreasonable."

I stopped. And turned. And looked at Lewis for the first time since leaving the bathroom. "What did you mean?"

He was watching me, his expression a bit cocked. "About what?" he asked.

"That I'd be unreasonable. What does that mean?"

"Only what I said."

"It's not what you said, it's how you said it. You thought 'I' would be unreasonable. As opposed to – ?"

"I don't understand what you're getting at."

"Are you pulling this shit on somebody else?"

"Eric, don't be ridiculous. Now, we're done here."

Like hell we were. I leaned against the wall and stared at Lewis. "You are. He's done it, again, and you're trying to scare the other guy off, too. Holy shit! He's done it, again! I TOLD that bitch he would! I told her! But did she listen? Oh, no!" I began to laugh. I was probably close to hysterics.

"That is completely and totally incorrect!" he snarled. "There have been no other charges filed against my client! None! The sole stain on Mr. Barrow's record, Eric, is from your malicious attempt to – !"

"It's Mr. Larson, you fuck," I snarled back, "and you're fucking lying! You think I don't get how careful your choice of words is? My father's a lawyer! 'No other charges filed.' So fucking what? Unless somebody else is thinking about filing them! Unless he got carried away and killed somebody and you're afraid the cops'll remember me!

Unless he did it to a kid and mommy and daddy're close to figuring out why junior's grades have dropped from A's to D's, all of a sudden!"

Lewis shook his head, in disbelief. "Allen warned me you were unstable," he said, almost gently. "I thought he was being melodramatic. I believed you would see the reason and logic behind my request. It looks like I thought wrong."

Man, if this was an act, it was a good one. The line was read just right. Shock. Surprise. Sadness. All melded into one simple statement aimed straight at what little was left of my sanity. A "reasonable" man appealing to another reasonable man even while acknowledging that reason was no longer a commodity in the room. It cooled my verbal fire.

"He covered himself good, didn't he?" I said. "If I agree to do what you want, I'm a blackmailing whore who got beat. If I don't, I'm nuts and should be committed." I looked at the woman and smirked. "What do you think, Ms. Calvert? You've been sitting over there all nice and quiet and observant, noting everything like a good little witness. What's the female take on me? Nuts or a skank?"

She looked away, not at all happy. Lewis stepped between us. "She is here solely as an observer, Eric."

"To back up your version of our meeting."

"Bluntly, yes."

I noticed the video frozen at showing me pulling my black slacks on (I thought I'd exited it; I must have only hit "pause"). My shirt was buttoned. My facial expression was that of a drunk old man. Allen was behind me, "helping." I strode over to the T-V, took the remote and pushed it backward at 12x, jerking us both into a crazy backward ballet of wild ludicrous movements. Why? I have no idea. It's hardly like that would make this easier to take. It was more like I was torturing myself for some reason.

Except.

Except I felt a need to see it, again. For some deep down reason. Because something about that project (aside for the whole disgusting idea of it) was off. Was wrong in some way, and I couldn't quite figure it out.

"He's done it, again," I said, almost absently, "and you're protecting him. Like the D-A protected him. Like the cops protected him. What I don't get is, why? Why believe him and not me?"

"Eric."

My image stripped and hopped back on the bed, spread-eagled facedown, as Allen un-unmounted me and fucked me in quick rabbit-like thrusts. If only it had really happened that fast. If only it had seemed so funny. If only he had taken the gag around my neck and twisted it until I was dead; the agony would have ended that night. Still, nothing unexpected here.

"Can I ask you something?" I said.

"Let me guess. You'd like to know how I sleep at night."

"No, I already know how that works." And I did. Dad filled me in. There were plenty of people in the world who could blow up a busload of school kids, slaughter people taking refuge in a church, hell, strangle a cute and cuddly kitten and then drift into a peaceful slumber. Why? Because they had no souls. And looking into that man's eyes, I finally understood what Dad had meant. People like Lewis had the same concept of morality as a cockroach or flea. And he would have the same confused response as them at being asked to justify actions that needed zero justification.

You see, Lewis was just giving his client the best defense he possible could. Just like a pit bull. Never mind that the pit bull's jaws are tight around a five-year-old boy's neck; the boss still needs protection. And he wouldn't want me to let go, would he? Get real.

No, what I wanted to know is, "How can Allen afford you? Your breed of attack dog isn't cheap, and he can't be THAT well off; not the way he dresses. So how's he paying you?"

"It's not a question of payment. It's a question of being innocent in this country until proven guilty."

That made me chuckle, "Bullshit. Lots of people're guilty until proven innocent. As you've just proven."

"I have no idea what you're talking about," Lewis said.

The tape was at the point where I was face up and Allen was PopPopPopPopPopping his little head on me. It was so cute.

Cute!? Fuckin' cute!? The very idea roused anger in me. Anger against me for having thought it. But at the same time, a cold clear logic was telling me there was nothing here to satisfy kitty's curiosity, either. So what was I looking for? Why was I keeping that hideous group of images flashing 'cross the screen?

I kept talking. "Simple. Woman gets raped, people still think it's partly her fault. Commentators snipe about how women dress. Where they go. Situations they put themselves into. Look at that girl who accused Kobe Bryant a few years ago. Ripped to shreds. Threatened with death. Gossip and tabloid headlines filled with lies and hate. And if she'd been killed, his defense would have painted her as nine kinds of whore once they got hold of her background. Only if she proves to be clean and innocent and virginal can she then be considered a true victim."

"That is patently absurd, especially in this day and age!"

"Shit, what're you doing? Running for office? It works both ways, you fuck. Look at what happened to those frat-holes at Duke. They even got ripped by national black leaders. Called racists and scum – and no apology when it turns out the woman was lying. Just, Guilty, guilty, guilty – oh, <u>not</u> guilty? Oh, well – nevermind."

My Dockers appeared back around my ankles and I flopped back onto the bed. My hands were back behind me, my shirt tangled about my wrists, the gag shoved back on my mouth. Then I was in the van, again, and struggling. Then I was walking backwards down the sidewalk on Melrose. In my black jeans and white shirt. And I slipped into the restaurant.

And then, as the preachers cry, "I saw the light!" It flooded over me like boiling clouds of knowledge. I hit the "play" button and watched myself exit the restaurant. And "paused" it. I suddenly had the sensation of having been on a rollercoaster one too many times, and I was about to shoot into the whole ride, once again. It was a giddy, almost drunk feeling that I was powerless to control. I mean, seriously, I wanted to do anything but understand this idea that was suddenly pounding at the back door of my awareness. But I had to accept it. I had to. And I also had to do something smart – keep my mouth shut.

Which I did. For a moment, anyway. Long enough.

I cast a glance at Ms. Calvert. She looked back, almost hurt. I smiled at her. She did not move. I used every trick I knew to keep my voice nice and casual as I said, "You're not just a witness, are you? You're recording this. Straight into your laptop."

Lewis sighed, long and hard. "What if we are?"

I punched the "eject" button. The disk popped out and I "absently" picked it up. "Getting into some legal gray areas there, counselor."

"You intend to lecture me about the law?"

"It's just, I thought it was illegal in the State of California to record someone without their knowledge, or getting their permission, first."

"A typical layman's assumption as regards a complex issue."

"Then our yakking is all on the record."

"Would you like a transcript?"

"Yes. And a copy of that release, too. Make it all official."

I walked to the door as calmly as I could, disk still in hand. I had it open and was about to leave when he said, "I expect you to drop the charges in the morning, you know."

I stopped. And I looked at him. And despite myself, I said, "It's not raining."

"Is rain expected?" asked Lewis.

"That night. It was raining, that night. And cold. That's why I got in his truck."

16

"I do not care about your explanations."

"And I'm in jeans."

"Listen, it's been a long night..."

"At the beginning. I'm in my black jeans. I wore those two nights before, on a Sunday. When it wasn't raining."

Lewis said nothing. I think he caught a glimmer of what I was getting at, because he had that diamond glare going, again. So I smiled. And stupidly happily filled him in.

"He planned it. He taped me leaving the restaurant two nights before it happened. A nice steady shot. Probably on sticks – that's a tripod. Slick zoom and follow with a decent lens. Very professional-looking. Does he do this for a living? Is that how he makes money enough for you? He never did tell me what his job was."

"Stop it, Eric," Lewis said with fake patience. "You both planned it. He taped you leaving work that night. And we have paperwork to – ."

"That's not what he told the cops." Lewis tensed. "And go back and look at how I'm walking. I'm pissed. I got bawled out for wearing jeans. Rene's harsh about that. Thinks they're unprofessional. I got away with it, Friday night, but he noticed on Sunday. I told him how I'd torn my only pair of black slacks. That they couldn't be repaired. But that didn't matter. He told me if I wore jeans to work, again, he'd send me home. I work there a year and a half without a complaint and he pulls a snit like that on me. I had to go buy a pair of black Dockers. The next day. And I had to wear them before I could wash and iron them because I couldn't afford to. Rent was coming due. When they did the rape kit, they kept 'em. As evidence. Had blood on 'em. A brand new pair. I still have the receipt. For tax purposes. I can back it up. All of it."

I looked at Ms. Calvert. She was watching me. Her PowerBook was still open. Excellent. Lewis stepped closer to me, that leopard's glare in his eyes, again. But I didn't move.

"You know what that means," I said. "He stalked me. He planned it. He came into the restaurant intending to find some way of getting me to talk to him. Let people see us together."

"You are extrapolating a new theory from nothing – ."

"Don't you get it?! I didn't lead him on! It wasn't anything I did! He'd already marked me as the next guy he was gonna have fun with! Him and his buddies!!"

And there it was. Stark and cold and clear. They planned it! Planned the whole thing to look like I was a trick Allen had picked up and paid to play sex games with! His defense, just in case I proved "difficult." There was nothing in me that secretly wanted him to rape me, to punish me, to even fucking touch me! And that bit of video at the beginning showed it! I kissed the disk!

"So you taped your encounter over two nights?" growled Lewis, "All it shows is a simple problem with continuity. Which proves nothing."

"Who gives a FUCK about what it proves to you?" I giggled. "That cunt of a DA had me all but convinced that I asked for this to happen. She said I just got pissed 'cause I didn't get paid enough for it. And it's not true. None of it. He stalked me. He fuckin' stalked me and he forced me to do it with him and this proves it! Proves it to me!"

Lewis grabbed for the disk. I ducked into the hallway, still giggling. He bolted through the door, after me, his eyes blazing. I gripped the disk like it was made of gold and danced away from him. He was nowhere near scaring me, now.

"I don't know how he made this fucker," I laughed at him, "but I'm glad he did! It backs me up! It backs ME up! And as for that fuckin' paperwork – I was drugged! It's in the tox-screen. He could've gotten me to sign the fuckin' Constitution, if he'd wanted to! So you go ahead and press your fuckin' false report charges, Mr. Lewis. See what the fuck happens."

He looked like he would gladly rip my head off and shit down my windpipe. "That DVD is my property, Eric!" he snapped. "If you take it, I will charge you with theft!"

I just kept giggling. "Fuck you," I yelled as I raced for the stairs. "Fuck you! Fuck you! Fuck you!"

I staked out the County Criminal Courts Building for three days looking for Ms. Elizabeth Ionescue, since the bitch wouldn't return my calls. I couldn't get inside; I had no jury summons or criminal case to contest or be part of, that sort of thing, and security was too uptight for me to slip past. So I just waited, haunting the rear parking lot's east entrance and exit, pacing before the driveway that curved underground from the street, figuring eventually she'd show.

Man, that part of downtown has such a 60's Futuristic feel. I'd paid minimal attention to it my last time down here, and now I had time to understand why. The big ugly buildings done in a governmental non-style. The wide parking lot sloping down the hill to slap up against a nothing "park". The few puffy green trees bisecting the lot, probably meant to mitigate the stark black asphalt but succeeding only in seeming pathetic. People of every race, color and creed heading up the stairs and around the ramp, entering and exiting without the hint of a smile or even the idea of simple human warmth. Didn't help that we were having a June gloom cycle in mid-August. Heavy days under thick clouds with threats of occasional rain, softening but not eradicating the heat. LA might not get as muggy as Minneapolis in summer, but it could damn well try.

I had nothing to do while I waited there except watch and stay alert. And think. No, actually AVOID thinking. I kept my brain distracted by memorizing each and every gleaming granite block of LA's City Hall, all done in soft gray – and less soft, depending on where repairs were made from the Ninety-four earthquake, I guess. Columns and arches were spaced clean and neat in that 1920's Deco-Greco style (whatever it's really called). Nice landscaping, if not spectacular. An aura of history radiating from it, along with near humanity if something like that can be ascribed to a building.

God, when I think of all the movies I've seen with those lean polished walls topped by more columns and a short-stack-style pyramid top as an establishing shot ("See, we're in Los Angeles, folks"). It once stood alone on the north edge of downtown. Near the 101. Towering over the city. Lord and master of its domain. Elegant in a way that was probably never truly intended. Now it was dwarfed by the gleaming new skyscrapers of Bunker Hill and hemmed in by pseudo-modern glass blocks used to house the ever-growing bureaucracies. The big gray whale of Cal-Trans and a bright cold-looking police headquarters were the latest to join it.

It's funny, but I caught a sort of proprietary attitude about that area. I found myself picking up trash and taking it to one of the overflowing dumpsters, nearby. I rubbed out what graffiti I could. I commiserated with City Hall's fall from its graceful dominance. Like I was telling it, "I understand, and I will be here for you. For this is my home, now, and I feel a strong responsibility for keeping it clean." How stupid.

On the third day (Wednesday, if I remember right; yes, it would have been, since I started my haunting on Monday, "duh") it started to mist. Not much, just enough to wet my spirit. I had yet to see the bitch enter or exit once, not even by the security lobby. Maybe there were underground tunnels connecting the government buildings and she used those; I'd heard there was something like that in Houston. Maybe she was on vacation. Or off in another part of the city on another case where she could act like a decent person to that crime's victim; there are so many courthouses spread about this town. Maybe I was just wasting my time hoping for a face-to-face.

But then a Hummer H-3 (of course, in way-too-cool-for-you black) drove up the underground ramp and I saw her behind the wheel. Without a second thought, I jumped in front of the fucking beast. Fortunately (or not, depending on how you feel about me, by now) it stopped.

She didn't recognize me, at first, and looked a bit spooked. Can't say I blame her. I was soggy and somewhat crazed, seeming more like a Fourth Street junky than a rational human being – though I will admit that latter suggestion was never something of which I could consistently be accused. So I wiped the hair away from my face and smiled and called out, "Hi, Ms. Ionescue, it's Eric Larson. Remember me?"

She did. And her bitch expression slapped onto her face in a nano-second. She lowered the driver's window a crack.

"I'm calling Security, Eric," she said as she whipped out her cell phone. "So you'd better leave."

"I'm not going to hurt you," I said, holding my hands out so she could see I didn't carry a weapon. "I just want to share something with you. About 'Mister' Barrow." Then I leaned on her hood, keeping my hands visible and the beast from moving.

She finally took a good look at me and realized how much my appearance had deteriorated since our last get-together. She shook her head. "What're you on?"

It took me a moment to connect with her meaning. "'On?' Oh-oh, drugs! Nothing. I WAS pretty heavy into crystal, but I haven't had any in – wow, in over a week." And the simple realization jolted me. I honestly had not even THOUGHT about doing any since last Tuesday night, I'd been so focused on what this tape meant. I mean, I'd been wasted in college a few times, sure, but I'd kept myself clean since; didn't want to mess with the career track. But then came Allen, followed by this DA cunt dumping on me and it was like – Hint of a problem? Bring on the Tina. And it seemed that was the only thing that kept me going. Until I met Allen's lawyer and found a better reason to live – hate.

"Congratulations," she said in her snide little way, which brought me back to the moment, "you are completely clean. Now get away from my car."

Oh, the fucking bitch.

"He did it, again, you know," I snarled, still luxuriating my sudden sense of sobriety.

"Then take him to small claims and leave me alone."

"What? Oh-no, not to me. No-no. No, to somebody else. Somebody where even if he says it was consensual, it won't matter; he'll still have to go to jail."

"What're you talking about?" I had her attention, now, though just barely.

I walked around to the driver's door. "Y'know, I never realized that once a criminal complaint is filed it stays filed. I-I-I figured when you told me to fuck off, that cancelled it out. Turns out, that's not exactly true."

"Don't explain the law to me, Eric; I know it better than you."

"Then tell me why Allen's lawyer would threaten me unless I withdrew the complaint I filed against him?"

"You're the one with the imagination; you tell me."

Meaning, I don't give a fuck; you're still a fag who's full of shit. I'd have smacked her if I could have reached her. Instead, I decided to brutalize her with words.

"He's scared. He stepped over the line and now faces prison, and he wants to make sure my complaint against him is as meaningless as possible. Probably to better his chances of cutting a deal. That-that you dropped the case might only mean you didn't have enough evidence to convict. But if I 'withdraw' the complaint, his attack dog can better argue it was nothing-nothing but the vindictive act of a two-bit hustler who was pissed off he-he-he didn't get paid enough for a bondage video."

She blinked. "Wait – are you saying he videotaped what happened between you two?"

With a smile, I pulled out a copy of the disk and nodded. "He used at least three-three cameras. Though it could have been four. Kind of home-movieish but smooth enough. And-and-and rather neatly edited. Though you can do that on any computer, these days. I think he and his lawyer thought I'd be so freaked out by the realization. That-that-that it's all on video." Man, I was stumbling over my words (and my thoughts), but I couldn't focus enough to let my voice catch up with my brain, or my brain with my meaning. "They-they figured I'd agree to do anything they said just to keep it quiet. And I almost did. Yeah, almost. But they forgot. Forgot that I'm an actor. I've seen hundreds of movies. I notice things in them. Silly things. Silly things like-like-like continuity problems. Inconsistencies in clothing. Things like that. And what this video proves is, more than one man was involved in my attack."

I had her full attention, now. "How does it prove that?"

"See for yourself." I offered her the disk. She lowered her window and took it, tentatively. A slip of paper was tucked into the case. She pulled it out and opened it.

"Those are the points in the disk where you can verify my claim," I said. "There are-are six of them. First-first of all, there's the fact that they taped me leaving the restaurant on Sunday night. Different clothes. Not only was it not raining and I was in jeans, but-but check out the wife-beater t-shirt under my white cotton one. It shows up when I pass under a streetlight. Later, it's obvious I'm wearing Dockers and a Polo t-shirt, the kind with sleeves and a thick finished collar.

"Second, they show me tied up in the van while it's moving, and the camera pans over me and zooms in, and on one occasion when it zooms out, the shadow of another guy wipes 'cross one corner when the-the van passes under a streetlight. It's small and in the background so you really have to look for it. But it's there. Allen couldn't drive and run the camera at the same time, not from the angle it's on.

"Third, don't forget, Allen said there was no van. That he picked me up in his car. But there I am in the back of one. No question. No question.

"Four is when I'm tied to the bed. And-and-and Allen's working on me. The camera pulls back. Just a little. It's like the first few frames of a slow zoom that they cut out but didn't make certain that they trimmed all of it. Both of Allen's hands are visible. So there's no way he could be operating a remote.

"Five is the best one," I smirked. "It's also Alan's hands. You'll see some great close-ups of them. On me. On me. Holding me. Showing he bites his nails. To the nubs. Cuticles, too. But at the beginning. When he's groping me. In two shots, those hands are manicured. Very nicely. Almost to perfection. And the fingers are different. Darker. Stronger. More pudgy."

She looked at me, half-frowning. Looked like I was getting through. I kept running, barely taking a breath.

"And finally, I-I-I only ejaculated once. After 'Wrestler' had his rip-and-strip fun. After Allen got-got-got to work on me. So the only 'cum' shot they had to use was while I was at the foot of the bed, only half stripped. So when I shoot. About two-thirds into the video. I noted the exact time. You can still see shreds of my-my-my briefs around my right leg. They contrast to the sheet I'm on. You can tell that's the shot they cut into the ending. Where I'm completely stripped and bound to the bed. You'll notice how wrong my position is between the two angles. Compare it to Allen's version of what happened; I'll bet you he swears he didn't tear any-any of my clothing."

The mist was threatening to turn into a light rain. I barely noticed and could not have cared less. I was on a roll.

"Compare this whole video to Allen's statements. You'll see a dozen discrepancies. Flat out lies. What's really sick is, I think each of them. Each of them. Allen and his buddies. Each one made a-a-a video about his favorite fetish. Using me as their lead actor. And looking at this and considering how smooth it is, I'd say I'm not the first person they did it to. And now? Now I'll betcha ten bucks I'm not the last."

"I haven't heard of another man being sexually assaulted."

"Doesn't matter. It's happened. And my gut says they did it to a kid, 'cause you can't get out of having sex with someone who's underage, no matter how 'consensual' you claim it was. A high school boy, probably. In a different district or county. Grabbed him on his way home from school. Or a basketball game. Or a movie. A kid who's now fucked up for life. You might want to look into that instead of waiting to hear about it through the grapevine. Something like this may take a while to get to you, and I think the investigators would just LOVE to know a little more about Allen and company."

She eyed me. "You seem happy about this."

Like she fucking had the right to say that to me!?

"I'm not," I said. "And I am. That's how fucked up I've become. But what's great is, it's all in your lap now. Here is evidence that everything I told you was true, and if you'd just listened to me and done your job instead of being a homophobic 'twit' (I almost said 'cunt' but that would have only lost her), you might have stopped them."

"This doesn't change the circumstances of what you claimed, Eric. It only puts one more chit on your side of the table."

I almost lost it at that comment. "Man, you are a lawyer. Always right, never wrong, no matter how many hairs you have to split. The spirit of the law? Justice? Responsibility? Those are terms for romantic idiots. What matters most is shifting the blame. Well now it's in your lap, baby, and I really love that this is about to blow up in your face. But at least. At least. At least it still hurts me. I'm not so far gone that I can't still hope I'm wrong. That they haven't killed somebody."

"That, I definitely would have heard about," she said, absently. The possibility of a black mark on her career was finally glaring, even to her. She looked away and put her mind into all-wheel drive. She now saw the need to do some damage control. I could actually see all of it happening in her face.

"I really do hope you're right," I whispered. "Not for your sake, but for the sake of the poor guy who was on the receiving end of their fucked up game. Now let's see if you can call this one a two-bit whore."

She looked me. She now had her professional expression back on. "When did you get this?"

"Week ago, Tuesday. You'd have had it sooner, but you wouldn't return my calls."

"I'll look into it and get back to you. We may be doing something about your charges, after all."

She rolled her window up and drove away without even a fucking good-bye, let alone an apology. I just stood there. In the growing rain. Forcing myself to keep a grin on my stupid face as the Hummer whipped down the street.

Oh my God, I hated that bitch. At that point in time, I'd have done anything to bring her down. And if I'd just left it alone, it would have. Oh, she wouldn't have lost her job, but she'd have started carrying questions about her abilities once this case was settled, and her career path would have shifted. Maybe she wanted to be a judge, someday. Or go into politics. Become the DA for Los Angeles County. Well, now that might never happen. Baggage like this tends to make you look incapable and obtuse, especially to your enemies. It gives people a chance to have second thoughts. And she'd probably have stayed an ADA the rest of her life.

But being stupidly stubborn Eric (from both the Welsh AND Swedish sides of the family), I couldn't let things follow their natural course, oh no. No, now I was on a hair-trigger. If she even hinted at hesitating, I was primed to kill. I was beyond reason from feeding on an anger laced with a desperate need for revenge, and I was going to push and shove and make damn sure she got as fucked figuratively as I had literally.

Still, I was able to put my descent into chaos on hold for forty-eight hours. Seemed like a decent enough interval to give Ms. Ionescue at least a chance to do right by me and everyone else she'd fucked over. Just good manners, don't ya know. So I called her office Friday to get a progress report (if she had one). I left a message. Twice. Once again, she ignored my calls.

So that evening, I called Detective-Sergeant Grant. This time, I got straight through to him (he must not have recognized my name). He'd already heard about the video, which surprised me. Could that bitch actually be threatening to do something about Allen? But

28

when he asked if we could get together for coffee after he finished his shift, I caught a glimmer that maybe I was being too pessimistically optimistic.

We connected at a Starbucks near his station and he handed me a blended mocha. I knew better than to tell him I'd have preferred tea, that I don't drink coffee; I wanted him to be as much on my side as possible, right now. So I accepted it. I could be a shit, later, if I still needed to.

He wanted to chit-chat, first. "How's it been going?" and all that crap. As if he couldn't see how deep into hell I'd fallen. I had no patience for it.

"What'd the bitch tell you?" I asked.

He blinked. "What do you mean?"

"C'mon, Grant," I said, dumping the casual politeness. "You knew about Lewis and Allen and the videotape. Ionescue must have filled you in."

"Not really. She called, yesterday, to ask if I knew about it. That's all."

"Did you?"

He blinked, again. I think I offended him. "Listen, Eric, I know you're angry, but this is not – ."

"You don't know shit about me! Or-or-or what this means to me!" I was threatening to slip into babbling, again.

"Bullshit!" he snapped, his voice low and growly. The force of it jolted me into silence. "You think you're the only person this has happened to? I'm faced with this every day! Every fuckin' day! Then half the cases I investigate get dropped, and half the ones I wind up taking to the DA's office are rejected! And of the ones that do get accepted, half get plead out to a lesser charge! And that's out of the maybe one-fourth to one-third of cases that even get reported in the first place!"

"Bullshit!"

"Check the statistics! I'm not far off in my numbers. And do you think for one fucking second that any of those women feels one damn bit less violated than you?!"

Suddenly I felt a hint of shame. He's right; rape happens far more often to women than it does men (by most studies) and too many of them get treated just as badly as I was. I had no lock on self-righteousness. Which pissed me off even more, being made to feel like that. But I held it in.

"Eric, I work my ass off trying to get assholes like Allen put away for hurting people. Innocent people. People like you. Yes, you. I know you're not what Beth said, but I'm not the one having to try a case in front of a jury that hates to even THINK about sex let alone determine if it was wanted or asked for!"

Ah, yes. American Puritanism smacks us around, again. We may be familiar with the best way to make babies and have little trouble with it being used to sell us beer, mouthwash and the latest fall fashions, but please don't ask us to contemplate the reality of it except in the privacy of our own homes and on-line with "Hot-to-trot-babes-dot-com." Sex is not meant to be discussed in polite society. And don't you never mind that we're hardly that, anymore, especially if we're on the right end of the political and religious spectrum.

"Okay, I'm sorry," I said, still a bit pissed but now aware enough of it to let it ride. "I keep forgetting not everybody's like that bitch."

"Cut her some slack, Eric. She's got a caseload stacked as high as you are tall."

That cut the rest of my pissed-off-ness out of me. Dammit. But maybe Moritz was right; maybe I DID need to get some facts to back my attitude.

Grant leaned back, eyeing me, and shook his head. "Son, you are a train wreck. Did you call the people I told you about?"

I sighed and shook my head. "I-I hooked up with a-a-a counselor at The Rainbow Center. For a couple days. Friend of a friend."

He nodded. "What became your drug of choice?"

That almost made me laugh. "What didn't?"

He grimaced. "You want a word of advice? Talk to someone. I don't care who it is. Even just a friend. Let it out."

"I don't have any friends, anymore."

"Don't you?"

I shrugged. "I haven't talked to anybody I know. In months."

"Phones still work. 'Hello' is still a good start."

He was right. But I just sat there, gazing at that coffee I hadn't touched. Trying to form a coherent thought. For some reason my brain was just plain refusing to cooperate. I mean, yeah – all I had to do was pick up the phone and call Moritz or Rusty or Laila or Lucia, or even Gerrod. And they'd probably welcome hearing from me. Be happy at knowing I was still on the planet. I'd tried to do that, a few times. But the second I'd think about it, I'd slip into this inertia and wind up hours later still telling myself I should call them. Must be madness.

I think Grant finally caught a glimpse of the chaos in my world and realized that maybe, just maybe, it was just as bad as anyone else's he'd dealt with. He leaned over, patted me on the arm and said, "Okay, Beth was a bitch about your complaint. And yes, it looks like nothing may happen to resolve that, not for you. And it's obvious that you're hurting. But, son, you still have the choice as to whether or not this situation will destroy you or help you build an even better life on firmer soil."

Oh, for crying out loud, could he combine a more obnoxious pair of clichés? "What doesn't kill you makes you stronger." "Build your house on rock, not sand." Shit. I really expected better from him. Shit, from people in general. And yet, I knew he was only trying to help. What it did was jolt my brain into at least one solid thought. Something I'd wanted to know for a while. But I felt the need to be careful, here.

"Can I ask you something?"

He leaned back, wariness in his eyes. I think he thought he knew what the question would be. Still he shrugged and said, "Won't guarantee you an answer."

Fine, I could play by those rules. So I surprised him with, "How did you locate Allen?"

He hesitated. "Eric, I'm not going to help you get back at Barrow."

"I don't plan to." Grant didn't believe me, so I detailed it for him. "You seriously think I'd give the son-of-a-bitch ANY excuse to fluff off my accusations? Or-or hit back at me?"

That connected. He took a sip of his coffee then carefully responded, "Through the partial license plate you gave me."

"Ionescue said it didn't work out."

"Not exactly true. It lead me to a van owned by some guys who run a video shop. Legitimate stock, with a room in the back for their 'Adult Clientele'. Gay and straight."

I didn't like the sound of that, at all. "Did you look the place over?"

"Yes, and it's just a regular store, with current releases and classics and cult movies. DVDs, Blue-Rays, a few videos left over, and they're doing well enough to hire a couple people – male and female."

"Is that where Allen works?"

"No. He's the customer service manager for a lapel pin distributor." I must have given him a look of confusion, because he added, "They make special pins. Key-chains. Medallions. Wings to put on your pockets. For things like The Olympics. Rock concerts. Commemorative crap."

"Oh-oh, okay, I get it."

"But he is a customer at the store. One of the clerks recognized his description. He was due to return a DVD that evening, so I waited for him. Saw him. Followed him home and questioned him. He seemed very affable."

"As opposed to me."

"That's not what I meant."

I nodded. I knew better. "You check out the van?"

"I can't. No warrant. Besides, it's not Barrow's. He doesn't have access to it."

"You should see the video," I said. "Shows me in the back of one." He blinked. "Ionescue didn't tell you about that?"

"No." I let the information sink in. Apparently this put a whole new spin on things. "Eric, you have to understand, his story threw me. Made me wonder what was going on. I filled Beth in, and we decided to arrange the photo lineup, to make sure it was the right guy. And so she could gauge your reaction to Allen's photo."

"Didn't matter. She'd already made up her mind."

He hesitated. "I prefer not to believe that."

"You're too much of a good soldier, Grant," I said, sipping at my coffee, absently. And instantly regretting it. It tasted burned. Like charcoal. Made me fill a bit ill. Want to just chuck the whole thing and grab a Moroccan Mint Tea and go home and curl up with Jag.

"I'll check out the video," he said, softly.

And he would. He was a decent guy. Dammit. Again, I should have let things run their normal course. Grant wouldn't have let Ionescue off, not if he could show the two guys who owned that shop fit my descriptions. He would have forced the issue. Because I could see, hidden behind his eyes, I could see a growing anger. And his anger fed my need to know. "What happened with me. Has it? Has it happened before? With him?"

He waited to answer. Half to keep control of himself; half to let me see just how much thought he was putting into it. Let me build in my mind the certainty of what he truly meant. Then he said, "I can't discuss my other cases with you."

Of course not. "Before me? Or after?"

"Eric..." His voice trailed off. He looked away. Then he cast me a sideways glance. I gave him my best wounded-puppy look. Hardly fair, but this was war. He glared at me long and hard, then leaned in close and whispered, "You tell anybody I told you this, I'll call you a liar."

"Just between us." I raised my hand.

"Almost a year ago. A guy in the Fairfax district vanished en route to Friday night services and was found the next morning in an alley, in shock. Couldn't talk. Wouldn't let anybody touch him without a fight. We got him to the ER and they did what they could to calm him, but when his father got there, the old man shut us down."

"How old was he?"

"Oh, he was like twenty, twenty-one, but his father was a Hassidic rabbi. For me to force the issue, it would've done even more damage to the kid. And that's not my way. The kid's whole family – mother, brother and sisters – they were all angry with him. Said nothing would have happened to him if he'd been with them when he was supposed to. Hadn't been late getting dressed. I tried to reason with him – get him to talk to me, anyway – but it was a no go. What's sad is, they stayed angry with him even after seeing how bad off he was. Last I heard, he was in Israel, on a kibbutz."

"But he WAS grabbed by Allen and his guys?"

"I don't know. He said just one thing in the hour or so I was alone with him that even began to make sense. 'Blue van.' And he said it just one time. Never again. But when a blue van popped up in your attack, I remembered that and checked it out. However, I've found no other case like yours where a blue van was connected to it. So keep in mind, Eric, there's nothing conclusive, here. It's just my gut."

"But you think they've done it, again."

Again, the hesitation. "There's a case being handled by the sheriff's department sounds a bit like yours. Blue van. Three men. Young man disappears for several hours. But, and this is a huge one, he was brutalized."

"And I wasn't?"

"We're talking almost beaten to death."

34

"Oh, Christ." I folded my arms around me. "They're getting worse."

"That's what I wondered, so I contacted a guy I know in Robbery/Homicide. Detective named Roscoe. But he told me this case was a man who got caught cheating on his wife and was beat up over it. Which killed the link, so far as I was concerned."

"But now?"

"Things have come out since that make me wonder."

"Who is he?"

"I can't tell you that!" This time I must have looked pissed off because he continued with, "Besides, it wouldn't matter. He's flat out not talking about it. At all. So once again, all I have to go on is my gut."

"And Ionescue?"

"She contacted the ADA assigned to the case and compared notes. She thinks the similarities are just a coincidence."

"But?"

"But?" Again, he took his time to answer. "But I think he's the reason Barrow's lawyer went after you. For a while it looked like he was going to press assault charges if the guy was caught. Then he dropped everything. Cold. Last week."

"Lewis spooked him."

"No – Eric, forget it! That's all there is to it."

I tried to get more out of him, but he shut me down. Not another bit of info from him. I think he figured he'd told me too much, because he finally said, "Son, let it go. Seriously. Consider what those guys did to you then compound it twice over for him. The man's got a family, and he's already gone through a shit-load from people based solely on RUMORS, so nothing you do will make anything that happened, not to you or to him or to anybody, any better. Go back to your friend-of-a-friend. Get your life on track. Let it go. It's the only sane thing to do."

I just nodded. He was right; it WAS the only sane thing to do. We chit-chatted a little longer. Until he was comfortable about me, again. Then we parted and I went home.

And I called Moritz.

"Eric," he cried, "where've you been?"

"To the moon, Alice."

He laughed. He thought it was hysterical that I'd never seen a full episode of "The Honeymooners" but could still quote most of Ralph's lines. "God, you sound SO much better than the last time I saw you. You were like a zombie, back then."

The walking dead. What a perfect metaphor. But enough of that; it was time to cut to the chase. "You remember that guy you used to date? Worked for some paper?"

"USED to?" Moritz sniped. "He moved in, July first. I tried to invite you over for the housewarming."

"Sorry I missed it. Tell me – can he hook me up with a reporter?"

"I suppose. Why?"

"Because, Mori," I said with all the self-righteousness I could muster, "I got a story to tell."

And that's where my part in this evil play really takes hold.

"BOBBY"

Himori set the news conference up for Monday mornin', since the team was flyin' out that afternoon for Chi-town after a couple off-days. Starsky, Rizal, Judson, the P-T guy, and Ronnie said they'd be there, too. I dunno why they felt I needed all that much backup...but they had lots more experience dealin' with the press than me, so I was happy to have 'em. But now...now I'm thinkin' maybe they had an idea what was comin'. Ivan was there, too, but he stayed off the side, more like he was watchin' than bein' part of it all.

I got there early, feelin' good. Donna dropped me off and I kissed her, real quick, just like I've done hundreds of times. I had my bag with me, ready to go, and thought I'd ask a couple the guys to join me for lunch at this Greek burger joint 'cross from the stadium. I just knew soon as we got this over with, everything's gonna be fine, again. I'd be back in control, again. Top of the world, again. I got nothin' to hide. Nothin' to be scared of...'cept my own fuckin' brain. Shit, nothin' to be 'shamed of. Like that first shrink said, I made it through a nasty ordeal alive and whole, and that's what mattered most. Fuckin' idiot.

Himori set everything up in this really nice conference room. Comfy chairs for the news geeks to sit in. A long table with mikes in front. Plenty of power and connections for the video guys. Water,

water, everywhere in ice cold bottles. You'd think they's announcin' a merger or introducin' an acquisition or somethin'. First time I'd seen 'em go all out for just a press conference.

I met with everybody in a room, next door...and the second I saw 'em, somethin' felt wrong. Tanner and Judson were there, too. Wearin' suits. Plus Starsky and Rizal were dressed better'n usual, even tho' we're about to head out of town, and Jay and Ronnie were done up real clean when both of 'em are usually the biggest slobs on the planet. And they all seemed, I dunno – tense. Like we were about to face down some pissed off League Officials or somethin'. I felt like I was wearin' rags, being in jeans, sneakers and a tee-shirt.

I popped off with somethin' like, "Jeez, calling out the heavy guns, Himori?"

He sort of smiled and nodded with, "We just wanted to be there to back you up."

Tanner chimed in with, "You've had it easy with the press, for the most part, Bobby. This time might be different."

Which gave me a shiver. "What you mean, Chief?"

He give me this real serious look and said, "No one's talked to them about what happened to you. Not the police. Not us. Not the doctors."

"What's to talk about?" I asked him.

"Nothing," he says back to me. "But some reporters have suggested we're hiding something. Rumors have been running over the blogs and we've even received e-queries asking if the attack on you was really random."

I got this sick knot in the middle of my gut. I looked 'round the room and asked the guys, "What're they sayin' it is?"

"Most of them seem to believe what happened was a drug deal gone wrong."

"Bullshit!"

Ronnie come over and said, "Of course this is bullshit, Bobby." He's got this crazy Russian accent made it hard to get what he's sayin', half the time, but man he had good hands in a massage. "But the press, it loves this bullshit. It wishes for you to live in bullshit, so they may cluck their thick tongues and say how horrible you are to do what we live for you to do. What you can do about it?"

"I'm just warning you, Bobby," said Tanner, "there's some reporters out there who won't be asking nice questions. I want you ready for that. Keep your cool. Answer them as honestly as you can."

"Do not lie." That was Himori addin' on to it. "If they catch you in a lie, they will eat your breakfast, lunch AND dinner then ingest a laxative and shit it in your face."

That jolted me. Not so much what Himori was sayin' 'bout the press – shit, I already knew that – but how he put it. He always used such great English, and he's one of the few guys I knew who could put you down total without using a single four letter word. Ma met him once and fell in love with him, almost, just 'cause of how he talked. "Cultured," was how she put it. I'm thinkin' it's a good thing Pop was along for the ride, the feelin' I got from that moment. Weird.

But what's crazy-weird is, him sayin' it that way spooked me. Now I felt like I had to defend myself not just to the sports writers but to my coaches and the staff. "Guys, I got nothin' to hide. I got jumped by some assholes in a parkin' lot. I dunno who. I dunno why. It just happened. I mean, shit like this happens, don't it?"

"Yeah, Bobby. Sure." That was Judson. He didn't look like he believed me.

So then I'm wonderin', "Why're people sayin' this crap?"

"Because they're bored," Himori told me. Then he took me by the arm. "Come, let's go in. I want to be ready for the first question by ten a-m sharp."

I held back, suddenly really freaked out. I felt like I was about to dragged into a cage full of hungry lions and I wasn't ready for it. I started thinkin', if I don't go in there lookin' good, they're gonna use that against me, too. I opened my bag and yanked out a shirt with a collar. It was wrinkled but I still put it on, buttoned it up, tucked it in my jeans and yanked on a light jacket to cover up most the mess. Then I ran a brush through my hair, like I ever give a shit how it looks. I even popped a mint instead of gum so I wouldn't be chewin' like some prize cow while all these guys chattered at me. I figured, if I was gonna face down the jackals, I was gonna at least look like a guy who give a shit.

TRANSCRIPT OF
PRESS CONFERENCE 07/29

HIMORI: Thank you all for coming. I called this press conference in order to make a pleasant announcement. One of the best closing pitchers we've ever had, Bobby Carapisi, is coming off the DL. As you all know, Bobby was brutally attacked just over a month ago, during which he sustained serious injuries to his head along with severe lacerations, deep bruises and several cracked ribs. This kept him in the hospital for five days, during which he underwent a battery of tests and treatment. Two weeks ago, he finally received a clean bill of health from his doctors and returned to practice, with the understanding that he'd keep it light. We didn't want to exacerbate the damage to his ribs. Under the watchful eyes of Lou Starsky, our batting coach, Hector Rizal, our bullpen coach, Jay Arnold, our physical therapist, and Ronnie Venetsianov, who heads up strength and conditioning, Bobby has made remarkable progress in getting himself back up to speed. We tried him out against Kansas City and Detroit, and he performed so well, both Coaches Starsky and Rizal recommended he rejoin the bullpen. The team manager, Frank Tanner, and head athletic trainer, Walter Judson, concurred, so beginning with tomorrow night's game in Chicago, Bobby Carapisi – AKA: "Mr. Delivery" – will be back in the bullpen. Now we'll open up the floor to questions. Yes, Claussen, let's start with you.

CLAUSEN: I have a question for Bobby.

BOBBY: Yeah, uh...

CLAUSEN: First off, it's good to see you're back in shape, Bobby.

BOBBY: Thanks. I feel like diamonds.

[Laughter]

CLAUSEN: Have you heard anything from the police about an arrest...or arresting the men who attacked you? Are they close to identifying someone?

BOBBY: Well...uh...I don't really know. A couple detectives came by a coupe days back and I...I I-D'd one of the guys from some pictures, but you'd have to ask them if they busted him.

STARSKY: I spoke with the Sheriff's Department, yesterday. Apparently, since it's taken them so long to locate every one of the individuals responsible for the assault, they've decided to present their case to the D-A instead of making a direct arrest.

CLAUSEN: I don't get it. Why not just arrest the man?

STARSKY: I'm not a lawyer; you'll have to ask them.

HIMORI: Schilders.

SCHILDERS: Bobby, your recent performance in K-C wasn't all that spectacular. In fact, Starsky had to pull you after less than two innings.

BOBBY: I retired seven of my first eight batters.

SCHILDERS: Then had a meltdown and walked three in a row. Do you feel you have the control you need to begin relieving, again?

VENETSIANOV: If I may this question answer – I believe the performance of Bobby speaks well. He retires four of the batters he faces, on strikes; he pitches two into popping out on fly balls; and he even forces a double-play. Unfortunately, this is when his ribs begin to bother him. For anyone who suffers a cracked or broken rib, they know only one is needed to bring about very sharp and intense discomfort.

BOBBY: It was like a knife, all of a sudden, in my side.

VENETSIANOV: It will be very sharp pain, and sometimes can seem even as if it will gravitate down your body.

BOBBY: I thought I could work through it.

VENETSIANOV: Which does not work. I saw this and strongly suggested he be pulled. This was after the first walk.

RIZAL: Yeah, it caught us all by surprise, so I got Mifune working and as soon as he was ready, Starsky put him in. So you see, part of the problem was me not having a backup guy ready. Won't happen, again.

SCHILDERS: But doesn't that suggest he's...Bobby's not really ready to...y'know...join the rotation?

VENETSIANOV: Although the pain still is there after more than four weeks, it also is far less significant. We work on his endurance, still. I believe very strongly he will quickly resume his training at a level where it would be otherwise anyway.

JUDSON: Uh, don't forget, pitching involves major use of the trunk and arm muscles, so a quick return to it, even after a light injury, is difficult. And you have to practice every day to keep up your abilities.

CLAUSEN: Thanks for the lesson in physiology.

STARSKY: It was my decision to not bring Mifune out, immediately. I wanted to see how Bobby handled himself. What I saw impressed me. After his first walk, he shifted his stance and began using tricks to bring the batters into swings they wouldn't ordinarily take. You can't win against every batter just on strategy, but still, that last batter, he went three-two before his walk.

CLAUSEN: But he still walked.

BOBBY: Yeah, well, I...I really thought he'd go for the fast-break. So much for strategy.

TANNER: Listen, gentlemen, Bobby joined us with a great deal of talent. That's why he only spent half a year in Triple-A; when we saw what he's got, we felt it's better to finish seasoning him up against the big boys in a position where we can really test him out.

SANTIAGO: Isn't that dangerous, to use major league play to test a pitcher instead of to keep him in the minor leagues?

STARSKY: He wound up closing twenty-two games, his first season, with eleven saves. We saw real fast that he's got a lot of control and is quick on the uptake in strategy. Even if you don't agree with my assessment, his stats speak for themselves.

HIMORI: Renfield.

RENFIELD: This is for Coach Starsky – are you planning to make Bobby your number six starter, next season?

STARSKY: It's too soon to say.

BOBBY: Aw, c'mon, coach. I'll be good, by then.

STARSKY: Right now he's still my best closer.

HIMORI: Santiago.

SANTIAGO: I am Luis Santiago with "Revista Basebol." Bobby, do you notice any losing of command of the fast and away ball you have? You do not pitch it so much, any longer.

BOBBY: No, I don't use it as much, but that's more 'cause I don't want to get batters too used to my pitches, y'know. I like to mix it up, much as I can.

HIMORI: O'Donnell.

O'DONNELL: Bobby, I notice your position on the rubber has changed dramatically in the last couple outings.

BOBBY: Yeah, I...I still favor my right side, some.

O'DONNELL: Does that mean you'll be changing it, some more?

BOBBY: Maybe. I mean, I know I'm not back to a hundred percent, yet. Physically. My speed's not back up there, yet, so I do what I can to make up the difference. And even though strategy doesn't always work against a batter, it's still important to keep up on it, y'know, and make it part of every pitch. So I...I'm still shifting things around, trying things out. Doing what I can to make me even better when I'm up there.

JUDSON: We're working in some exercises to bring him back on line. Doing long tosses, too.

BOBBY: I can still own the plate.

HIMORI: Langston.

LANGSTON: Bobby, last season, your ERA was 2.65. This season prior to your attack, you carried an ERA of 3.16 with seven saves. The last two times on the mound, your ERA was 4.5 and both games were lost on your errors...

STARSKY: The Detroit game was lost on Coleman's error – .

LANGSTON: The error was assigned to Bobby.

STARSKY: Which was bull – uh, horse hockey. Coleman's the one who lost the pitch and let the runner come home.

LANGSTON: Looked like a wild pitch, to me.

BUSH: And me.

STARSKY: Even Coleman said it was his fault.

LANGSTON: Whatever your feelings about it, it raises the question as to whether Bobby's ready to come off the D-L. The Griffins are barely above .500 for the season, we're just weeks past the mid-season break, and his stats were already getting worse. Can the Griffins afford to bring up a pitcher who's out of control?

HIMORI: Who's your question aimed at, Langston?

LANGSTON: Bobby.

BOBBY: I...uh...I gotta leave decisions like that up to Coach Starsky and Coach Rizal. I...I think I showed, in my first two innings both times...well, the first six or seven batters...that I was at a hundred percent.

LANGSTON: But then your collapse was spectacular.

BOBBY: Listen, I'm not a guy who likes to give up, know what I'm saying? I keep pushing myself to do the job and don't like to admit that there's...uh, there's times when it's better if I stop and let somebody else take over, y'know. I never had something like this happen to me, before, y'know. The few times I...I been hurt before, I worked through it and did okay.

MAXFIELD: When was that?

JUDSON: Year before last, when we played Boston in inter-league. Bobby pulled a hamstring but finished out the inning and I sent Mifune in. He wanted to keep going but I wouldn't let him. I had to fight him to put him on the fifteen day D-L.

HIMORI: And he was still picked for the All-Star Game, Maxfield.

MAXFIELD: Bobby, are you sorry you weren't picked for the All-Star Team this year?

BOBBY: No. C'mon, the fans pick the guys they go for. I ain't been out there as much, this year. But we got a good bullpen going. Good rotation. Not as much need for me.

CLAUSEN: But now several of them are in slumps or are on the DL. Is that one reason you're rushing back into play?

RIZAL: We wouldn't put him back in if we didn't feel he could handle it.

HIMORI: Gentleman in the back...uh...?

INNOLIO: Fabio Innolio, "Dispatch." Bobby, do you think you still are in the running for a Cy Young Award?

BOBBY: Doubt it, but I can't think about stuff like that. I just do my job, best I can. If I get it, I'll be happy, but I don't worry 'bout it.

SCHILDERS: Do you subscribe to the belief that the best first pitch in baseball is "strike one"?

BOBBY: I like it, okay, but I'm still more for the old one-two, y'know.

HIMORI: Okay...uh...Channel Four, Weiss.

WEISS: Bobby, what's your opinion on the push for a salary cap?

BOBBY: I dunno. I love pitching ball. I'd do it, no matter what they paid me. Uh-oh – sorry, Ivan. Maybe I shouldn't of said that.

[Laughter]

CALDWELL: Who was your most influential mentor?

BOBBY: Hmm. Uh...jeez, I've had so many. I guess it's Coach Tucci, when I was in Little League. He's the one first put me on the mound, first made me think I could pitch good. That I had the arm for it. He's still coaching Little League, last I heard.

LANGSTON: Is it true that your relationship with Jones has deteriorated over the last year?

BOBBY: I got no idea what you're talking about. Jonesie and me, we work good, together. Fact is, I rely on my catcher. I feed off him. He knows things about the hitters I don't, and he's right there next to them, so he's got a better idea what kind of state they're in. I couldn't pitch as good without something coming to me from my catcher, and I've had some of my best games off Jonesie, almost as many as with Coleman.

HIMORI: Yes, Ms. Seymour.

SEYMOUR: Bobby, I understand you're close to becoming a father for the second time. How's it going?

BOBBY: Oh, uh...great. He's due in a couple months. Maybe three. I never can keep that stuff straight in my head.

SEYMOUR: So it's a boy?

BOBBY: Uh, yeah, this one's gonna be a boy.

RENFIELD: You have a name picked out?

BOBBY: Robert Thomas, after me and my Uncle Tommy.

GILLIAN: Bobby, do you ever get frustrated with your team's defense while pitching?

BOBBY: Why would I, Mr...?

GILLIAN: Gillian, "Baseball Express." It just seems that this season when you're on the mound, your teammates don't really try to back you up.

BOBBY: What you talking about? Any pitcher'd feel great taking the mound with this defense behind him. I mean, the guys...they back me up, y'know. They do their best and then some. Me, I could work more with my power and velocity, sure. But sometimes the other side's gonna get hits, no matter what you do. Most the batters I come up against're damn good at it. Me, my job's to keep that to a minimum. And the guys on my team bust their butts to keep them from scoring.

WEISS: Bobby, what're the chances of a Pennant, this year?

BOBBY: Oh, that's too far away from now for me to worry about it. You never know what direction the team's gonna go in, so I'm focused on playing my next game, and my next game only.

LANGSTON: What about the rumors on the blogs of you being traded?

BOBBY: I don't know jack about those.

CLAUSEN: Word is The Griffins're looking for some more pitching power.

STARSKY: Which is natural, considering our suddenly very lean bullpen.

CLAUSEN: Chang's a free-agent, this year. Would you be up for trading Bobby if you could get an arm like his?

STARSKY: No.

BUSH: While we're on the subject of rumors, there's one I'd like Bobby to address.

BOBBY: What's that, Mr...?

BUSH: Bush, "Cable Sports News." It's been suggested that your attack wasn't just a random incident.

WEISS: I've seen that on one of the blogs.

BOBBY: What you talking about?

BUSH: They claim the reason the police are reluctant to make an arrest is there's something of a more "personal" nature behind it.

LANGSTON: That's one way of putting it.

BOBBY: Guys, I don't get you.

HIMORI: Now, just a minute, just a minute. The web pages are full of unfounded rumors and ridiculous claims, gentlemen, and many of them fly in the face of facts. Even my son showed me one that swore Bobby had actually been kidnapped by aliens and taken back...oh... five thousand years in time to see how he'd adapt to...to...what was it... Babylonian sports.

LANGSTON: Which is ridiculous on its face. But what about a drug deal gone wrong? Such things happen all the time.

BOBBY: Drugs?! I don't do that kind of stuff.

LANGSTON: Not even steroids or any other performance enhancer?

BOBBY: No! Listen, I...I underwent a test not so long ago.

WEISS: Three days before you were assaulted.

JUDSON: And the results were completely negative.

STARSKY: He's set to take another one, before we leave.

LANGSTON: Why would you do that unless you were giving the reports credence?

STARSKY: I expect it will also be negative, so unless you have some reason to speculate otherwise...and so far you've shown none...let's drop it.

BUSH: Well, if everything's so innocent, Bobby, then why did you go to that particular store that late in the evening? Even the police have questions about that.

BOBBY: No reason. I mean, my wife just likes the place.

BUSH: Then why did the police also question Emmanuel Jones and his wife concerning his whereabouts on the night you were attacked?

BOBBY: I...I didn't know they had.

RENFIELD: When was that?

BUSH: While Bobby was still in the hospital.

WEISS: Whoa.

LANGSTON: Well...you have to admit, Bobby...I mean, your explanations about that evening have been pretty vague, so far.

BOBBY: What d'you want? I don't remember what happened. I went to that store. I come out to my car. I got clobbered. Next thing I know, I'm in the hospital. What more you want?

BUSH: A reason why you went to a store in the basin when you could have gone to a much closer store in the valley.

BOBBY: I gave you one. My wife likes to shop there.

BUSH: C'mon, how many guys even know when their wives buy groceries, let alone where they buy them?

BOBBY: She told me.

BUSH: And you paid attention?

HIMORI: That's enough, Mr. Bush.

LANGSTON: So, Bobby, the police haven't raised the possibility in their questioning of you that your assault may have been provoked?

BOBBY: Provoked?! For what?

LANGSTON: A drug deal gone wrong.

BOBBY: Why do you keep harping on that?

LANGSTON: Because the Sheriff's detectives handling the case were brought in from their Vice Detail.

BOBBY: What?

TANNER: Whoa, whoa, whoa, whoa, whoa, that division of the Sheriff's department also handles kidnappings.

CLAUSSEN: And prostitution. Interesting mix.

STARSKY: Okay, we're out of time – .

CLAUSEN: Wait a minute, I have another – .

BOBBY: Hey, I didn't do anything to provoke this! I love my wife and my kid and I wouldn't do anything to hurt 'em.

BUSH: What're the police saying to you, Bobby?

LANGSTON: Have they accused you of participating in any crime?

HIMORI: Gentlemen, thank you for coming.

SANTIAGO: Is this why there has been no arrest?

WEISS: Bobby, what HAVE the police told you concerning their investigation?

HIMORI: All future questions should be passed through my office.

END OF TRANSCRIPT

I guess it goes without sayin', 'stead of makin' things right, that press conference set a couple guys after my butt. Clausen, Bush an' Langston – Himori referred to 'em as a "triumvirate of evil" – I mean, it's like they had a vendetta against me from that point on. Like I was lyin' 'bout what happened an' they were gonna find out the truth if it killed me. Didn't matter what I said.

Now don't get me wrong. Most the reporters there were all about the game an' nothin' else. Their bits were decent, honest, wishin' me well an' hopin' the team made the pennant with my help. Fact is, Weiss even took up my side an' said I ought to be given even more space for a while, till the cops were done with their investigation.

But Bush...that asshole went after me hard. Writin' columns on how my pitchin' wasn't so great an' I was overpriced for what I was bringin' to the team. How I was lyin' 'bout what happened that night an' he knew it. He hinted at – never right out said, but kept suggestin' – that I was havin' a thing with Jonesie's wife, that he found out an' him an' his brothers from Baldwin Hills were the ones beat me up. Seems Bush got cozy with this lawyer handlin' Jonesie's divorce. I think I even heard somewhere they were, like, first cousins. Anyhow, it was this lawyer's way of lettin' the soon-to-be-ex-Mrs. Jones she better not ask for shit in a settlement or he'd cut her open a new one an' use me as the knife, an' too bad for me if it ain't true. They didn't have nothin' to back it up, but that didn't stop 'em from layin' it out for everybody to see.

Now I wanna get somethin' clear here – Jonesie's wife is a beautiful woman. Any man'd be nuts not to want her. An' I got the feelin', once or twice, she'd be up for doin' somethin'. Not so much 'cause she's a whore but 'cause Jonesie wasn't takin' care of her, know what I mean. That guy had some weird bullshit goin' on in his head 'bout how women should be treated. An' I don't mean he was all "gangsta" an' "whores" an' "bitches" an' all that; it's more like she's his property, just like his car. He decides when he wants to go for a drive; he decides when it's goin' in the garage. An' if he feels like somethin' new an' different, he's got no trouble rentin' a new one, know what I mean. But me, Holy Mary, I had a wife. A woman I loved. I'd never cheat on Donna. Never.

Jonesie, he got pissed about it. Called Bush a racist prick on video, which got lots of "beeped out" airplay. But it seemed like he was more pissed 'bout the idea he'd need help to beat me up – an' that he'd go an' be sneaky 'bout it – than the fact that it was me bein' trashed over his divorce. 'Cause you see, he never got rid of that lawyer that started the story. Never said he didn't think his wife an' me were a thing. Never even spoke with me about it. Hell, he wouldn't talk with me, at all. An' Bush used that to make his bullshit seem even more true.

Then there was Langston. Langston was after me on drugs. He was positive I was on somethin' that night or out buyin' somethin' an' the team was tryin' to keep a lid on it 'cause of the harsh new drugs policy from the commissioner's office. He shied away from talkin' to other guys on the team, at first; instead, he hit on guys who'd been traded. Guys like Lorraine. Who I think blamed me a bit for his trade, since I was doin' so good at the time he was slumpin'. Who'd spout off anything that come to his lame brain.

Lorraine told him 'bout this time at Colorado, when I had a cold the size of fuckin' Texas. I got so hopped up on Contac so I could be available for play, I got light-headed. Stumbly. Rizal had to pull me from the bullpen an' bring in Agebede, who wasn't as strong as me. We still won the game, but it was dicey the last inning. Anyhow, Lorraine'd made a crack wonderin' if I'd been poppin' Quaaludes 'cause I was so dopey. Word got back to Judson an' he wanted to take a blood test to make sure they hadn't signed up some kind of junkie. I let him do it, I was so scared if I said no they'd pull my contract.

When Ivan found out, he flipped nine ways from Sunday an' went nose to nose with Tanner, who tried to out scream him, but it didn't do no good, 'specially when the test come back showin' all I had was somethin' you could buy at any drug store. Lorraine still called me the team junkie for a while till I caught on how to handle him; I let him know if he didn't cut it out, I'd tell everybody the last chick who'd sucked him off was named George. He told me I could suck his dick an' I shot back, "Why'd I wanna do what you already do so good?" Which didn't make a shitload of sense...but it made the fucker laugh an' he left me alone after that.

Till Langston came callin'. Then it's me back to bein' the team junkie.

Man...that prick strung that one goofy incident into an indictment of how baseball hides its drug problems. An' I was his poster boy. He'd decided I was knocked around by my pusher for not payin' for some blow or horse or crank or whatever shit was the hot horrible thing of the moment, an' the cops were helpin' cover it up. He said he got hold of a "confidential" hospital report showin' I hadn't been as bad hurt as everybody claimed. "Two cracked ribs, a mild concussion, some minor cuts and bruises and he's kept in the hospital for five days? In this day and age of 'kick you out the second you can walk' medical care, what could possibly warrant a longer stay than overnight? Perhaps Mr. Carapisi was kept incognito so as to give him time to 'decompress' and 'withdraw' from the more immediate stages of a drug dependency." Yap, yap, yap.

Good thing is, Judson an' Tanner an' the doctor handlin' my case ripped him a new one for it. They called him an idiot an' deliberately dumb an' went after him for violatin' my doctor-patient privilege. The hospital even came down hard on him, wantin' to find out who gave him a peek at my file, an' he rolled 'cause he knew he'd gone too far. Turned out he'd paid this girl in their accounting department five thousand dollars to give him a copy of the initial ambulance report. All that happened then was, she got fired an' he got even more publicity for his claim, which he never took back. Mainly 'cause the hospital refused to release the results of blood tests done on me. Made me sick.

But the worst was Clausen. Him and Weiss worked Roscoe in tandem, tryin' to worm out of him what he really thought happened. An' Roscoe let just enough out to make Claussen buy into his pet theory – that I was a fag who got caught steppin' out on his fake wife an' kid. Oh, he didn't say that right out, no. He just hinted at it. Suggested I was hidin' somethihn' way down deep. Even from chief an' Himori an' the guys on the team. He was a sneaky bastard.

But Weiss, he wound up on my side after Roscoe let slip how much he hated queers like me. That made Weiss do some of his own investigatin'. He talked to Springer – Claussen never did – an' watched the store's security tapes. Then he went to the first store I stopped at an' got them to show him their tapes, which showed me goin' straight to the ice cream section an' lookin' an' comin' away empty. The cops hadn't even done that. He interviewed the old lady who said saw me get grabbed, an' she wasn't near as batty or unsure as Roscoe let on. Yeah, she was lookin' away when I got to the car, but she heard the van's door open an' looked around an' saw me gettin' pulled in the truck. She was headin' inside to tell somebody when she was almost hit by the van as it raced off the lot. He come away with a whole different idea – that I WAS kidnapped an' beat up, but it was by some guys who THOUGHT I was queer. Seems there'd been reports of gay-bashin's in West Hollywood an' Silver Lake over the last year an' neither of the cops'd tied those in with what happened to me...but Weiss did an' it pissed him off.

I got the word to watch Weiss' show week after the news conference, an' he went all hell after both Claussen AND Roscoe. He showed the tapes, the old lady's interview, police reports, an interview with the E-R doctor, everything he could think of an' come to the conclusion a couple of homophobes were trashin' the reputation of a guy who'd just been in the wrong place at the wrong time. He ripped 'em for "tabloid sports journalism" an' questioned the sincerity of the sheriff's department when it come to investigatin' hate crimes. It was beautiful.

His comments got picked up by the cable news shows an' a couple sports channels an' even the blogs started fightin' over it. Himori said it was like nine-to-one in my favor. Reporters started showin' up on my doorstep – well, at the security gate; guards were under orders not to let anybody in – to ask me what I thought about it all, an' I made sure I stopped an' talked with 'em as I left home or got back. Same at the stadium. I was Mr. Nice Guy all over the place. Anything you wanna know, just ask. An' I backed up what Weiss'd said – that I figured I was just in the wrong place at the wrong time. He'd tossed me a lifeline an' I made full use of it.

Claussen huffed an' puffed in his column, but he finally let it drop. Same for Langston. So many people started askin' why they had it in for me, they even had to explain their takes on the story.

As for Bush, he kept at the "me an' Jonesie's wife" angle for another week, even sneakin' past the guards an' surprisin' Donna on our doorstep. He asked her questions like, "Did she know I'd been cheatin' on her?" an' "Had I been sneakin' out a lot before the attack?" an' shit like that. She slammed the door in his rat-face, called security an' they dragged him off, but he was still screamin' questions the whole way.

I was on the road when she called but I still almost got on a plane to come back an' kill the motherfucker. I mean, shit, Donna's six months pregnant an' that asshole's tryin' to keep his fucked-up story alive by screwin' with her?! Son-of-a-bitch! 'Stead, I called Aunt T an' she come over to be with Donna. She also called a buddy of hers at the Teamsters, an' that buddy called the magazine Bush wrote for an' let 'em know if the little shit bugged my wife, again, they'd have a strike on their hands. With pickets. Bush shut up, after that, lemme tell ya.

After we got back from the road trip – we'd done pretty good; won six out of nine – I met with the District Attorney at Gino's, this restaurant in Hollywood; good eggplant parmesan an' I'd swear their sausage is home made...which wasn't a good idea since I'd packed on a good 30 pounds the last couple months. Well...twenty-five, 'cause I'd gone back on Aunt T's way of feedin' me and dropped a few. He filled me in on what the cops'd come up with...which wasn't too much.

The guy I I-D'd was named William Allen Barrow – "Wheel" Barrow; fuckin' figures. Worked for a company that makes those little pins you get, like flags for your collar an' ribbon pins an' stuff, know what I mean. He had an old Lincoln he drove around, not a van, an' he swore he'd had nothin' to do with me gettin' beat up. He was at the store an' saw the van pull in as he left, but that was it.

"That's not what Roscoe says he said," I popped off.

The D-A nodded an' sighed. "What Detective Roscoe told you was his own idea of what happened. He said that to see what your reaction might be."

"An' Springer went along with him?" I asked him.

He nodded, again, an' was all, "Unfortunately, Detective Springer thought his partner had re-interviewed the subject, but learned later that he hadn't. That it was all supposition."

"Then all that shit he told Claussen – ?"

"Was unacceptable." He cut me off, an' then he added, "He has been reprimanded for it. I apologize on his behalf. Just between you and me, Detective Roscoe has been in Vice for so long, he believes everyone involved in a crime, be they victim or perpetrator, is either a junkie or a whore or both.

"Now we've reviewed all of the evidence we have, the medical reports, the witnesses and security tapes, and we have very little to go on. There is no question you were taken forcibly. The mere fact that you left a gallon of ice cream to melt on the roof of your car, coupled with how one of your sandals was left behind and that a witness corroborates your version, is more than enough evidence to show you were kidnapped. However, you have no recollection of the events as they transpired after you were struck, and the men who attacked you left behind minimal forensic evidence. Even swabs taken of your face and mouth and – ."

I jolted an' snapped out with "Hey, hey!" I was so quick an' sharp about it, he stopped an' looked at me, frownin'. Then he got this gentle look on his face an' nodded. Again.

"I understand," he says. Then goes on with, "The partial license plate we culled from a video capture references over a hundred similar vans in the Southern California area, alone, many of which are owned by businesses whose employees are authorized to use them, and even have keys to them. So, to put it succinctly, unless you have more information you can share with us, our investigation has reached a dead end."

Meanin', they weren't goin' to do anything about it. An' what's really funny is, I was glad. I wanted it all gone. All behind me an' twenty years in the past. Kill the beast 'fore it kills you, know what I sayin'. So I smiled. Maybe even chuckled. An' I said, "Good."

"Are you sure? Because if you wish for us to proceed..."

"End it. Please, just end it."

He said, "Okay," an' that was that. He told me he'd keep the file open and' make like they were still makin' inquiries, but once the dust had settled, he'd put the file away an' we'd let it die. He was a nice guy an' very apologetic 'bout not bein' able to do anything more, but I was happy it was over. Happy I could get back to rebuildin' my life.

An' things kept lookin' up. My ribs got to where they only bugged me a little, so my next three outings as relief, I shut their guys down. Rizal made it clear to the whole world, if I'd been pitchin' a straight game, I'd of had a no-hitter. Made me feel like diamonds. What was even better was, I started hittin' good, too. I mean, I'm no Hank Aaron or Mark McGwire, that's for sure, but I batted in a couple runs an' even scored once, myself, on Coleman's Grand Slam against Chicago. It felt top o' the world.

At home, things weren't great, but they were better. Donna an' I kept separate rooms, an' I still had to kick back a couple shots to relax myself into sleep, but I started noticin' the dreams weren't comin' so much. The mornin's weren't so hard to get out of. The times I lost focus, I started bein' able to count on one hand. End of my third week after the press conference, I started tryin' to hit the pillow without a shot. If that didn't work, I kicked back just one. An' it seemed to be okay. Donna said she'd still hear me mutterin', sometimes, but I didn't remember any of it, not like I had before. So that was better, too.

An' I had better control of my temper. It took focus, lemme tell you, but Priss got to where she wasn't so worried 'bout if I was "good daddy" or "mean daddy", anymore. An' my fights with Donna all but quit. She even started lettin' me touch her, again. Nothin' sexual, y'know, just...just lettin' me put my hand on her shoulder without flinchin'. Runnin' my fingers through her hair without pullin' away. Glidin' her into a hug without havin' to pull her. Holy Mary, it was feelin' so good. I started thinkin', I can make it out of this. It's been more'n three months of hell, but I can make it back to bein' me.

Then...as I arrived for a game with Seattle...Chief called me into his office. Himori was there. Both of 'em looked like death warmed over, an' the first thought in my mind is, They're tradin' me. If only.

Chief had me sit on the couch...an' he joined me. That really got me scared. He saves talks like this for really bad news. Like maybe I was gonna be sent back to triple A. I wasn't ready, at all, for what he started sayin'.

"Bobby, I just got a call from a reporter at the Times. He's been trying to reach you but hasn't had any luck." No shit. I don't answer my phone when I'm home 'less I know who it is. Chief kept on with, "He's doing an...an in-depth article on...uh...he's investigating the police response...and District Attorney's response to...to what happened to you."

I went like ice. I could barely say, "What you mean?"

Himori chimed in with, "Apparently a young man...a waiter-slash-actor claims he was sexually assaulted by the same man – uh, men who...um, attacked you. He reported the incident and was brushed off. He saw your case was also being ignored, so he convinced the paper to look into it."

I got that weird edgy feelin', again, like just after I'd been hit. I couldn't speak. Couldn't even look at either of them. I sort of noticed Chief fold his hands together in his "fatherly way," and lean closer to me.

"Bobby...I want you to know something. I'm not just the team manager, right now. I'm here as your friend. As someone who will support you, no matter what. And I mean that, son. We know the hell you've gone through in the last three months and we will do our damndest to protect you from more of it. But I need to ask you. I have to know. Truthfully. Honestly. Because that reporter is asking the same question and...and hinting he knows the answer. So please, son, tell me. When...when those men attacked you...did they also...also abuse you...sexually?"

Suddenly my heart was poundin' out like I'd run 'round the bases a hundred times. I couldn't breathe. Couldn't think. Couldn't even really see. I stood up...an' two blinks later, I'm face down on the floor an' Himori's screamin' into the phone for Doc to come while Chief's kneelin' beside me, freaked out. This time, I broke my nose for real. I sort of remember seein' blood on the carpet as Chief rolled me over. I think I smiled at him. I'd like to think I did. Let him know, It's okay. It's not your fault, Chief. It's just me. Just me. Just me. But then this wall of black surrounded me...an' I slipped straight back into hell.

I woke up out of this nightmare...what it's about, I didn't know... but I did. I...I was back to that night, back to all the shit those bastards were doin'...and what's crazy-weird about it is, I...I...I knew what they were doin'...everything they were doin'...but I...I didn't, y'know. I mean, I'd get flashes of it, and know exactly what it was and where they were... they were...their hands were...where...uh...everything was an'...an' shit, but I'd sling it out of my mind so fast, it didn't really register. If that makes any sense. But it seemed like it went on forever till I slammed myself out of it an' opened my eyes an' saw Doc standin' over me an' some hideous strong smell tearin' my nose apart. Stung my eyes, too. I started heavin'.

Doc rolled me on my side, an' that's when I saw I was lyin' on Coach's couch an' Doc was actually kneelin' next to me, sayin' real soft, "It's okay, Bobby. Deep breaths. Come on. Breathe deep." He started rubbin' my back, strong but gentle, an' kept on whisperin', "Slowly, Bobby. Nice and slow. Easy. Breathe deep. Nice and easy." Till I was back in control. Took a bit. Somethin' about it...it didn't sit right...got me feelin' scarier. An' that's crazy. It's just Doc. Bein' Doc.

My head was killin' me, poundin' away like I was gonna have a stroke or somethin'. Doc must of sensed it, 'cause he asked, "You want something for pain?" I guess I nodded, 'cause then he said, "Okay, roll onto your back. Stay down."

He rolled my sleeve up, slipped a needle in my arm, an' I started feelin' it work within seconds. Damn, it was good. He pulled up a chair by the couch, watchin' me as it took away the pain an' keepin' me from tryin' to sit up.

"Not yet, Bobby. Lie still a while longer."

I didn't argue. I rubbed my face and felt tape on my nose. Doc shrugged. "Yes. I reset it. We'll see how it turns out."

That's when I looked around an' saw nobody else was in chief's office. I looked at doc an' he smiled, "Tanner and Himori are talking with Hirstadt. Nothing to worry about. Just contract nonsense. I'm to join them soon as your aunt arrives."

"Aunt T?" I got worried and went, "Where's Donna?"

Doc smiled as he said, "Nearly seven months pregnant. Do you really think it's a good idea for her to drive all this way in that condition?"

I just sighed and rolled over on my side, away from Doc. I understood what he meant, but I was still hurt by it. I thought things were gettin' better between us, again...but maybe they weren't, after all. Which was a stupid-shit selfish thing to think. I knew how hard it's been for her, carryin' this kid in the middle of all this crap...an' I'm still wantin' her to take care of me like she's got nothin' else goin' on? What a bastard I was.

Then doc dug in on me with, "Bobby, why didn't you let me know?"

I didn't react, really, 'cept to say, "Know what?"

"What happened to you. I spoke with Donna. She referred me to the physician who attended you in the ER. He didn't want to speak with me, at first; mumbled something silly about you demanding the report be kept private. But your wife let him know that as your doctor I'm entitled to know everything that happens with you, so he filled me in. Even faxed over his private report. Son, why couldn't you trust me with this?"

I had no answer. Doc's taken care of me so good all five years, even in Triple-A. But to tell him...to let him know – shit, I couldn't even face the idea Donna knew, so how could I tell anybody else? I just lay there.

He kept on with, "You know, I've been taking care of athletes since before you were born. I've handled all sorts of situations, from drug dependencies to venereal diseases to heart attacks in kids barely out of college to steroids complications to even teaching a few of our players simple hygiene. I've also dealt with more than one who was in a situation similar to yours."

Say what? I shifted 'round to look at him.

"One had been abused by his high school coach. All four years. The man told him that's the price he had to pay for being on the team. To say his self-esteem was minimal is to make an understatement. Another was assaulted while pledging for a fraternity. With a carrot, which he was then forced to eat. A third – well, he got a bit too drunk, one night, and awoke to find himself face down with his best friend – his married best friend – on top of him. In the middle of a pennant race. Which his team lost, which he blamed on himself for letting himself get raped. All of them manifested pretty much the same psychological reactions as you're obviously suffering from, now – denial, confusion over your sexuality, fear, nightmares, drinking too much."

"You ain't kiddin', you talked to Donna," I muttered.

He nodded and was all, "After listening to you murmur in your sleep, for a few minutes. She said she's been trying to get you to see a therapist. Why haven't you?"

I told him, "I was handlin' it."

He come back at me with, "On your own? Son, why would you do that to yourself?" I didn't answer him, straight off, so he kept on. "Do you seriously think you deserve to be punished for what happened?"

I told him, "I should of gone to a store in the valley."

He popped back at me with, "Why?"

I shrugged, "Cops said so."

He huffed an' went, "What a stupid fucking thing to say to anyone! Especially someone who's just been through a trauma like yours."

"They didn't believe me." An' then I spilled everything to Doc. About what Roscoe an' Springer said. What the guy that I I-D'd said. What the DA said. I didn't feel a thing while I said it. Just words comin' out, that's all. An' when I was done, that was that. No weight off my shoulders. No sudden awareness of how I can take back my life. Nothin' but Doc sittin' there an' me starin' at the ceilin'.

He finally nodded and asked me, "What do you want to happen?"

I wanted it all to go away, like it never did happen.

Doc sighed and said, "That's impossible. But we can make it livable. First off, I want you to talk to a friend of mine at the Rape Crisis Center. I'll give you her number. There are many different ways of handling this sort of problem, Bobby, and she's the best person to help you find out which would work for you. Secondly, I think you should disappear for a while. Get away from LA. Go someplace no one can find you. Take your wife, not your child. You and she need to reconnect. You cannot get through this without her. So talk to her. Be honest with her. Re-open the lines of communication you once shared and learn to rely upon her, again."

"But the team..."

"I'm putting you back on the DL. Fifteen days, for now, thirty if I have to. I want you incommunicado, and not just so you and Donna can have some privacy; when that article comes out, there will be a number of angry sports writers coming after you, who will be feeling betrayed because you did not come forward with such a personal matter during the last press conference. Never mind that it's really quite diseased they wish to dissect your private trauma in front of the whole wide world; they will be vicious. Especially the ones who stood up for you against Claussen, Bush and the others."

Holy Mary, didn't that make me feel even better?

He kept on with, "Had I know the details of your assault, I would never have allowed the press conference to take place. But it has, and I can handle them, Bobby. I've kept those bastards' noses out of more lockers than you can even begin to think of."

That's when I asked Doc about what happens after. I wasn't thinkin' 'bout it, really. Didn't want to. Really. But Doc assured me everything was gonna be fine. Seems Ivan was talkin' with Himori an' Chief about extendin' my current contract by five years. I'd be kept as a closer, never get to be a starter 'less I kicked so much ass, people couldn't pay attention to anything else. But I'd get to keep playin' ball. All it needed was my an' Doc's okay, so I gave it and so did he; I knew a good deal when I saw it.

Fact is, I was grateful for chief allowin' me that. He could of cut me loose. Damaged goods, know what I mean. 'Stead, he stood behind me. They all did – Ivan, Himori, Starsky, Rizal. 'Course, I ain't some fool; I knew part of the deal was I had to pitch good. Damn good. Damn fuckin' good. They even had me set up for an early back. In three weeks we were slated to play Cincie – Cincinnati – in inter-league play. Rizal said he'd use me to close at least one of the games, since they didn't really count in the standin's, an' Cincie was a fairly easy town to play in, right then.

So I went along with Doc's prescription. Soon as Aunt T dropped me back the house, I called that lady he was talkin' bout and she seemed lots easier to talk to than that guy I'd been referred to, first. She said she'd make space for me to come in soon as Donna an' I got back, an' she told me to keep in mind – I didn't ask to be attacked. I didn't want it. Nobody had the right to do it to me. I was the one got victimized. I was the victim an' that's all that mattered. She told me to keep tellin' myself that when I was gettin' too lost, an' when we got together, she'd help me find my way back to control.

Then I bundled Priss off to Aunt T's. I talked with her 'bout it while we drove back from Pomona an' she was all up for it; even said we could use her place up Lake Tahoe. She's got this house with a perfect view of the lake; I'd been up once, before, when I visited from college. Hadn't had the time, since. Nobody knew about it an' it couldn't be traced through her; it was in Raymon's company's name as a business property or somethin' like that.

Holy Mary, that house really was the perfect place to be. It fit in this sharp hillside like it'd been formed there, all stone an' slate roof an' big open windows. Trees all over. A deck with nothin' under it for a good two-hundred feet, then a creek bouncin' down to the lake. Fresh breezes flowin' by. Nearest neighbor was who-knows-where-an'-don't-it-feel-good-not-carin'. I told myself, once things settled down, I wanted a place like this. A sanctuary.

Donna didn't say a word all the drive up. Fact is, she seemed to sleep most of it. I'd caught the feelin' she wasn't too crazy 'bout the idea of bein' in the middle of nothin' nearin' her seventh month, but she come with me. I took that as a good sign.

She'd been quiet with me a lot, lately...like she's waitin' to see what's gonna happen, next. Or like she don't know what to say. An' she did look awful tired. Aunt T noticed it, too, so she got Raymon to let us take his new Chrysler 300. His baby. It's an easier ride than my truck an' there's no friggin' way I was goin' near that fuckin' Mustang. I made up for it by lettin' him use my Dodge. What's funny is, he laughed when he started it up; said it made him feel like he was back in college tryin' to prove how butch he was.

Aunt T laughed with him, sayin', "Baby, I think havin' four sons is plenty proof of your butchi-ness."

Even I laughed at that one. Donna, at least she smiled. Then we kissed Priss bye an' headed out.

Holy Mary, that car was nice. Still smelled new. Seats that fit you but weren't too hard. Everything right where you'd want it. Took maybe a thousand CDs an' played 'em on a sound system I'd be proud to have in my home. An' it purred up the Five, just like Uncle Tommy's old Charger'd do, hittin' down the Turnpike. Set the cruise an' you could float wherever you wanted to go. So when Donna closed her eyes goin' over the Grapevine an' didn't open 'em again, practically, till we were on the Eighty-eight, I wasn't really surprised; one just like it would of been perfect for her.

We got to the house close to midnight an' crashed. An' we spent the next couple days just putterin' around. Doin' nothin'. Not even talkin'. Donna cleaned the place on the inside, an' I cleaned up the outside. We picked up groceries in Stockton on the way up so didn't need to go anywhere. We just kept busy doin' thing to keep from facin' each other.

It had satellite, so we had all the sports channels. News channels. Anything I wanted. I steered clear of 'em till Saturday, then I started checkin' 'em out to see what was what. First blip I got was durin' this afternoon ballgame, where one of the announcers asked his color guy if he'd read the story in the early edition of the Sunday paper. The guy said, no, he didn't read the Sunday paper till Sunday. So the first guy tells him to check out the article on page one, column one.

I had my laptop with me, so I went online an' checked out the paper's website. I had to sign up for it, but I was able to read it...print it out...do anything I wanted. So I downloaded it, sat on the balcony overlookin' the lake an' read it.

It wasn't bad, really. The writer was real careful talkin' about what happened, an' to start off, he focused on this other guy – guy named Eric – who'd been grabbed goin' home from work. Ranted on at how little the cops an' the DA's office had done in response to it. Talked loads about how the guy'd crashed into drugs and gone into prostitution in reaction to the legal system's neglect. Got doctors an' therapists to discuss Post Traumatic Stress Disorder in tons of detail.

Then he got to the guy who'd been one of the guys who...who did it to him. Little Allen Wheel-Barrow. Who swore he'd paid the guy – Eric – for sex. Didn't know anybody like the two guys Eric was describin'...who sounded kinda like the guys who...who'd been all over me. Had a good job but now he was afraid of losin' it an' was goin' broke with lawyer's fees an' crap. Yap, yap, yap. But I had to say – he sounded good. I'd of believed him if...if he hadn't...if things'd been different.

It was him denyin' he'd even been part of what happened to me that lead into talkin' 'bout me. "Just a guy in the wrong place at the wrong time," he said. Over an' over. This Eric guy was usin' my "misidentification of him" to try an' get money out of him. An' that's all he focused on – that I'd seen him in the store an' later, when I got my brains bashed in, I'd picked him out the lineup for no real reason. What happened to me was tragic but he had nothin' to do with it.

By this point, I'm thinkin' maybe I DID make a mistake. Maybe the only reason I picked him was 'cause he'd spooked me in that store an' then I'd been sacked on the head. I'd never got a good look at the guys once I was in the back of that van. But then the whole tone changed.

This writer compared the city-wide search for me with how things were handled after I was found. There was the APB, the hundreds of cops lookin' for me, the media blitz that was like an Amber Alert. An' then nothin' once I was in the hospital. The FBI asked to look at the Sheriff's files an' were told not to waste their time; it was just an assault. No hate crimes involved. No nothin'. Just a guy who happens to be famous got beat up. So what? We handle that shit all the time. No big deal.

Except the writer then took hold of Roscoe's theory an' used that to suggest the Sheriff's Department had decided that since this crime had homosexual implications, it shouldn't be followed up. An' he wondered why, since it meant lettin' three thugs keep on doin' what they were doin'. Then he pointed out the silence that surrounded me once I was out of the hospital. Pointed out how slow the investigation was goin', an' how the DA's office was rumored to be about ready to put the whole thing on ice. He dissected that press conference and made special mention of how it'd been cut off when the questions got too sharp on what'd happened that night. An' that's when he laid it out. It was to protect me. To keep people from findin' out what happened to me. What really happened to me.

Now he never specifically said he knew what'd happened to me, that night. It was all suggested an' hinted at, but you could tell what he was meanin'. An' on top of everything else, he made it sound like The Griffins were part of this...this huge conspiracy to protect one of their home-boy's money-makin' ability at the expense of all these other little guys, who had no way to protect themselves. He cut especially close when he ended one section with, "If two women had come to the police with complaints of being attacked by the same group of men, the legal system would have moved mountains to keep it from happening, again, sports franchise or no sports franchise."

I couldn't read anymore, after that. I closed the laptop an' went inside to get myself a brewski. I popped it open and went back on the balcony an' watched the lake, far below. Lots of green and some gold and brown mixed in with the gray and white rocks. About four layers of mountains in every direction. Hawks and swallows flyin' around all day; owls flyin' by at night. Boats whipped by on the water but you couldn't hear 'em. It was like livin' in a bubble, I thought. Nobody to bug you or make you face life or anything nasty if you don't want it. Doc was right to send me up here.

The sun was startin' down to the left...to the west, so I was lookin' north, starin' at this old redwood tree 'cross the ravine from the house. There'd been a nest of eagles in it, last time I come here. I remembered bein' all hopped up about seein' 'em comin' an' goin' like some five year old kid. Aunt T'd got a real kick out of it. But now it was just there. Tree was probably hundreds of years old. And I wasn't thinkin' about anything...and I was gettin' peaceful.

Then I heard Donna comin' up behind me. It was like she was on tip-toe, tryin' not to make a sound, but I knew it was her. She's my wife; I know everything there is to know about how she moves and stuff. Like when she's tryin' to be sneaky, she has this little shuffle. Like she doesn't take her feet all the way off the floor when she walks. Like that'll make her quieter. It don't. Anyway, she stood behind me and I could feel her starin' at me.

I broke the quiet for her with, "What time is it?"

And she's like, "After seven. You hungry?" I could hear the tension in her voice, hear how she's tryin' to get the nerve to say somethin'. I nodded. "What you want?" I shrugged. "Soup?" I shrugged.

She sighed. I could just see her expression – Jeez, why don't you just tell me, for cryin' out loud? Then I heard her sit on the lounger an' say, "What you were reading on the laptop – was it that article?"

"Yeah."

"May I read it?"

I asked her, "You really need to?"

She took a minute to say, "No. But I'd like to."

An' there it was. She let me know, for sure, that she knew. And what's funny is, I knew from the beginnin' she knew. But I couldn't pull it together in my head to really, I dunno, accept that she knew. Till she said it. I didn't move.

She kept on, made herself say the words. "That doctor told me all of it, while you were unconscious. Gave me some numbers of people to call. People to talk to. He...he said I ought to get you to somebody, fast. A therapist. But I have to tell you, Bobby...I didn't believe him. I couldn't figure out how a guy can do that to another guy. I mean, I knew...I had an idea, but...but to you? To my Bobby? You're not that way. It didn't make sense."

I could hear her tryin' hard to keep steady and calm, keep from cryin'. And I wanted so much just to turn to her...but I couldn't move. No matter how hard I tried, I couldn't make myself even so much as twitch a muscle. I felt like I was floating above it all, waitin'. Waitin'. An' then it came.

"Unless...Bobby, I have to know something. Are...are you gay?"

What?! Boy, I looked 'round at her then. "How can you ask me somethin' like that?! Didn't the doctor spell out what happened to me!?"

"Yes, he did. Because he wanted me to let him do a rape kit on you. A rape kit! On you! I told him that he was crazy, that you'd never let another man do such a thing to you!"

"You think I LET 'em do it!?"

"I don't know."

"Holy Mary, you think I...I...?!"

"I don't know! That...that's why I'm asking."

"Why? Why're you askin' me that?"

"Because...because he talked me into it. Into doing the kit. And he told me what he found. There were only traces of one man on you."

But there were three of 'em on me. Three. One after the other. Fast an' hard an'...an'...holy shit, back away, Bobby. Back away. "Donna, don't. Please."

But she kept on. "But that's not all of it, Bobby. And he told me it didn't mean anything."

Holy Mary, I knew what was comin' next, I knew it, I knew it, I could see it happenin', again, an' I was all, "Please, Donna, don't."

But she kept on. "He told me you...you ejaculated."

"No-no-no-no-no-no."

"Yes, Bobby. There's no question about it. He found your own semen mixed in with – ."

"STOP IT! I can't fuckin' believe this! You think I WANTED IT! You think I'm like that! All this time...when you took me to that priest... when you sent me to Father Matt...you knew! An' you thought I had somethin' to confess to?! You thought I wanted it?! What the fuck you think I did, Donna? You think I beat myself up to hide it?"

An' she's backin' away from me, now, scared. "No," she's sayin', real soft, "no...I...that's what's so confusing about it all. That's why I have to ask."

"HAVE to ask? HAVE to fuckin' ask!? You don't know me well enough, by now!?"

"Well, you did have that uncle who was queer and – ."

I hit her.

I froze to the spot. Blank. Floatin'. Not a thought in my head 'cept, I hit my wife. Oh, Jesus, Holy Mary, I hit my wife. I hit Donna. I mean, it wasn't a fist, I didn't use a fist, my hand was open, it was really a slap...but-but-but it was a hit. I hit her. I fuckin' hit her.

I caught a glimpse of this other thought...'bout how quick it'd be to just step back a few feet an' tumble over the railin' an' float down to the creek an' end this fuckin' nightmare. I half thought I'd wake up 'fore I hit the rocks. But I couldn't move. Couldn't breathe. Couldn't even really see. I was just shredded inside by the idea that I'd hit my wife.

I didn't have to see Donna to know her expression. Some kind of mix of disbelief an' pure out fury. She might have been ready to tear into me, screamin' an' scratchin' like some crazy-assed freak...but she didn't do a thing. She just stood there. Like I stood there. Maybe she was tryin' to think of what to say or was as blank as me at that moment. I dunno. She didn't say a fuckin' word.

All of a sudden, the wall was smashed, an' I whispered somethin' like, "They made me like it. They...they forced me."

She was real quite, for a minute, then she said, "Forced you?" She had this snarl in her voice.

"Yeah," was all I could say.

"He forced you – .

"THEY, Donna. Three of 'em."

"All right...three men forced you to have sex with them, and made you enjoy it."

"I didn't enjoy it!"

"You just said they did!"

"He...they...they took me off. That's all."

"That's all."

"Yeah. I...I dunno how they did it...but...but..."

"But they turned you queer?" She said it so matter of fact, it cut deeper'n anything I'd ever been told before. "He turned you queer." Plain and simple.

I popped out with, "No!" but she was gettin' angrier by the second.

74

"Then what're you saying!? You just told me that you had sex with a man and you liked it!"

"I said, he made me! I didn't want him to but – ."

"Listen to what the fuck you're saying, Bobby! You can't force a man to enjoy being raped! Unless that's what you're into."

I had to look away. I mean, she was right. Maybe. I mean, yeah, maybe you can make a guy get a hard-on. Said so in that article. Those doctors were talkin' 'bout you how can...when you do some of the stuff those bastards did to me...you can make him...make him...shit. But how can you get him off if he don't want you to? That don't make sense...unless he turned me queer.

That's what it boils down to: If he made me like it, then maybe I wanted it. Maybe I'm a closet case, like Claussen keeps sayin'. I must of got into somethin' more than I wanted and I got found out and now I'm cryin' rape. Cocksucker. But maybe he's right. Maybe they all are. I can't argue, not now, that I didn't...I didn't...aw, shit, I still can't say it.

I mean, I never even thought about bein' with a guy! Not once, in my whole life! I swear it! Yeah, I've heard stories about some ballplayers not carin' whose lips are on their dicks so long as they're gettin' off, but I wasn't into that. It made me sick. Shit, the only time I even let Donna do it was when she was carryin' Priss and my right hand wasn't handling it, anymore. And that was only once or twice.

I like...love girls. Ever since my first time with Angie Quinn my junior year in the back of her dad's Lincoln. Holy Mary, she was hot. Tits out to here. A nice ass for grabbin'. Lips that you could kiss for years at a time. Golden hair down the middle of her back. We made that car buck for half an hour. I still got a scar from where her nails dug into my back, and I still can get hard just thinkin' about her. Would a gay guy still feel that way?

I never looked at the other guys in the showers. Not once. I mean, not to look. Yeah, we horsed around and made fun and snapped towels and made so many jokes about droppin' the soap, they weren't funny anymore. There was a couple guys I wished I looked more like – tight like Gary Molinarsky or lean like Juan Cardenas – but only 'cause of this layer of fat on me that I can't get rid of; not 'cause I...I was after them. I never even compared dick sizes 'cause I know Donna liked mine just fine and that's all that mattered. So why the hell did I...did I get off on it? How'd he make me like it?

But I didn't like it. Not really. Didn't really feel it...except to know it happened. And I heard him gloatin' over it. Sneerin' at me. He said, "Took you long enough, baby," then punched me in the gut and got down to...to more of it. And I hated all of it. Everything he did. None of it was right for me; all of it hurt like hell. Still hurts...at night.

But that didn't matter, right now...not to Donna. Now she was off on a screamer. "So how many other guys have you done it with?!"

I wasn't even thinkin', just then; I just yelled, "None!" right back at her.

Man, she was red in the face and she was still screamin', "Then do you want to?!"

Right below the belt. By this point, I knew I shouldn't of admitted to it and I tried to take it back by tellin' her, "No! Donna, I swear, that ain't my way and – !"

She broke me off with, "You just told me it is!"

"I meant that he got me off! That's all! I didn't want to, but he did! And I don't get it! I don't get how he can do that to a guy who don't want to and...and...and it's got me so screwed up!"

She bolted away from me. Started pacin'...which is a good thing. When she paces, she's thinkin'...and she's not just screamin'. I tried to catch her eye, show her how...show her...shit, I dunno, just show how much I wanted her...needed her to believe I was tellin' her the truth.

"Baby, listen to me – I don't get it. They beat the shit out o' me. Tied me up. Did things to me. Made me do things I...I can't even think about, yet. I was so scared. Prayin' to God He'd let me see you and Priss, again. Prayin' He'd let me live to see my son get born. And...and I dunno how it happened, but it did. Maybe they gave me some kind of drug. Like Viagra or somethin'. Not just that...the ones they advertise, but things you can buy on the street an'...an'..."

She shot a look at me and she's like, "DID he give somethin'?"

The way she asked me. Like, prove it. Tell me or I'm fuckin' out of here. So I lied to her, and I'm like, "Yeah. A...a coke, I thought. I was real thirsty...and my mouth was so dry...and..."

I couldn't say anything more. He never gave me a damned thing before it happened. The coke came after. After. I gotta be honest 'bout it, now. I wouldn't of been so messed up over it if he had. I'd of had that to hold onto, too, like it was somethin' in the coke. But I can't. He just knew what buttons to push and how hard to push 'em...and he ran me like a train. But it gave Donna something to hang onto.

"Wait." She stopped an' looked at me, hard. "I never found out the results of the Toxicology test. The C-B-C. That doctor never told me..."

"He told Doc. Gave him everything."

She went back in the house an' grabbed the phone. I could see her punch in a number. She spoke soft so I couldn't hear her...but I knew she was callin' Doc to verify my lies. I didn't move the whole time. Just watched her through the window. Watched her listen to him. Watched her relax into the idea. She finally hung up an' come back to me.

"Viagra and ketamine," she said.

That hit me. It's the same crap that the other guy – Larson – said were found in him. But of course they found crap like that in my blood. I felt it start up seconds after that sip of coke. I mean, I'm lyin' there...hurtin' like hell an' so glad for just a sip of anything...an' soon as it's in me I can tell it's got somethin' in it. I ain't stupid. That's why I started fightin' back so hard; I knew they were gonna do even worse to me, then. Maybe kill me. That's why I bit that son-of-a-bitch when he tried to make me – I...I bit him hard. An' I hurt him, I know. I can still taste his blood, sometimes. That's why the other two tore into me so bad...to make me let go...an'...an'...aw, shit.

Shit.

But the good thing was, at least...at least Donna was back to sayin', "Why didn't you tell me?"

And I'm like, "I couldn't. Couldn't even say it to me. Couldn't even believe it happened to me. I...I couldn't. I just couldn't let you think that I...that I...I..." and then I saw this big red welt on her face an' I knew I did that to her an' I went off bawlin', again. Standin' there like a big slab of stupid, tears screamin' down my face, shakin' like a baby.

It took like forever, but Donna finally put her hand to my cheek and drew me close and gave me her shoulder, an' I let a river run down her back...soakin' her nightgown...an' she's like, "Okay, Bobby. C'mon, Bobby Boy, it's okay. It'll all be fine. It will. We'll get you some help. Get you somebody who can help. It'll all be fine."

An' I believed her. I needed to believe her. An' I really think it would have been.

It would of been...except there were a pair of assholes hidden behind that redwood, tapin' it all. They had this tiny-assed video camera pokin' between the branches with this big-assed lens that gave 'em a perfect scope of me an' Donna. An' a mike that'd pickup a cricket at a thousand yards. They heard every word. Every fuckin' word. An' ten days later, the supermarket rags were all yellin' the same thing – "Bobby C Confesses To Wife: I'm Gay!"

I called Ivan day after the Times article hit an' asked how things were goin'. He told me he had good news; that Doug Weiss, the guy who'd backed me up, some, was open to interviewin' both me an' Donna for his Sunday Night sports show. Give us a chance to face down the rumors an' accusations an' crap that were flyin' 'round, but in a safe settin'. I wasn't too crazy 'bout it; I didn't want more attention focused on my wife, not the way she was feelin', right then. But Ivan talked me into at least askin' her.

What surprised me was Donna was all, "Fine. It's time to hit back." Didn't even stop an' think about it.

I'm lookin' at her, the kid stickin' out to here, an' I'm thinkin', "Are you sure? It's still gonna get rough."

An' she's all, "It'll be worse if I'm not with you."

We went back an' forth on it, for a while, 'fore I called Ivan back an' told him to go ahead an' set it up. He did, to tape on Friday.

Things actually got better, after that. Now that Donna had somethin' to hold onto. Me tellin' her I was junked up made it okay with her. No...no, that's not the right way to put it. It's not like what happened was okay; it's just...it was just...just understandable for once, to her. She wasn't so sheltered she'd never seen smart people do stupid things while on stuff, before, an' then not be able to explain why. One of her brothers even admitted to her once that he drank so much, one night, he blacked out an' then drove home like that. He stopped drinkin' over it, it freaked him out, so much. An' it didn't hurt Doc'd verified what I told her.

We never talked about me hittin' her. I never said I was sorry. She never seemed to want me to say I was. It's like we both decided without words that it's better to be ignored than faced, right then.

But I still felt like a dog over it. An' on top of that, I was hurt from knowin' Donna knew. Knowin' she knew everything the whole time I'm goin' through this an' not tellin' me. Holy Mary, that...that was somethin' I...I couldn't accept. I'd always done right by Donna. Cared for her. Provided for her. An' Priss. Never a rumor 'bout me before this. I mean, not about cheatin' on her, y'know. I'd been true to her, no matter what. An' then this happens...an' she wonders if it's true? If the worst is true? Doesn't even talk with me about it? She just goes off wonderin' if...if I'm the kind o' guy who don't care whose lips are on my dick, like it doesn't mean nothin'?

Why? I don't understand why. I can't understand it. Unless it IS somethin' in me that other people see an' I don't. Like Father Jacks. Like that little ass-wipe, Barrow. Like Roscoe an' Clausen. Like even the DA, maybe. Maybe they all look at me an' see somebody who could be queer. Who could want what...like what...what happened to me. Who could get off on it. Who could be got off from it.

An' that's what really gets to me. No matter what I say or think or do, I can't get past the one real truth of this whole thing – they got me off. After all three of 'em...all three of 'em did...did that.

Aw, shit...

One of 'em took me off. I'm lyin' there, hurtin' an' bleedin', sick from what they did to me, thinkin' I'm gonna die...an' one of 'em took me off. How can you do that to a guy unless the guy wants you to?

I didn't know what to think. I still don't. Just knowin' Donna... she thought I...shit, it makes me sick, inside. Makes me want to hurl.

Even now. An' back then? I couldn't face it. Couldn't accept it. So I shut it out. Focused on gettin' my life back on track. I had to. Had to make sure I could keep my career an' make a bit of cash to live on. I...I couldn't let somethin' like this sidetrack me from what mattered most – takin' care my family. Not right then.

So I let things get better. For Donna. Did whatever she wanted. Smiled at her lots. She got back to fixin' me Aunt T's recipes to cut back on my weight gain, 'cause I was closin' in on two-forty-five. An' she pushed me back to workin' out, sort of. She'd talk me into goin' out for a run an' I'd do it till I was out of sight, then I'd just walk for miles an' look at the views an' think about nothin'. She was back to bein' my wife, again, I guess. After wonderin' if I even wanted one, anymore. I let her keep on bein' that way. Holy Mary, I needed her to be back to that way. Just till I could get back to LA an' see that woman Doc told me about an' see if she could explain what the fuck happened to me.

'Course, I still slept on the couch. Didn't want to risk wakin' Donna with more dreams. 'Cause they were back to poppin' up. 'Sides, it let me sit an' drink an' spend a couple hours tryin' not to think till I drifted off to sleep. Made me feel like shit in the mornin's, but it was better'n facin' life, right then.

An' it's not like I had to keep it up for all that long. We drove back down to LA on Thursday an' checked in a hotel near the studio for the night. I'd spent all week textin' Ivan 'bout the show an' questions Weiss'd ask, an' I talked with him on the phone for a couple hours once we got checked in, so I used that as an excuse to not sleep that night. Donna said she understood an' went on to bed.

Me, I went up the pool on the roof an' went swimmin'. At one in the mornin'. Nobody's supposed to be there that late, but nobody said nothin'. Man, I really pushed it. Goin' back an' forth. Doin' the Australian Crawl an' the Butterfly an' shootin' underwater from one end to the other. Pretendin' ol' Uncle Tom-Tom was there watchin' over me. Wishin' he was. He'd of had the answers I needed. I know it. So I just kept on swimmin'. Back an' forth till I wore myself out. I think I finally crashed on the bed at three.

Next day, we hit the studio at noon. Word'd got out about the show an' some reporters were at the gate, tryin' to get me to say somethin' but I drove on past. Didn't even listen to any of their questions.

Ivan met us at the door with one of Weiss' producers, a girl named Renate Horst-somethin'-or-other. She lead us to a waitin' room, sayin' stuff like, "Doug'll be down in a minute to say hello," an' "There's nothin' to be worried about," an' crap. Donna used the bathroom then sipped at some juice as Ivan an' me went over some last minute stuff. Seemed Bush'd dropped his original idea 'bout me sleepin' with Jonesie's wife, now that she had a new lawyer that was just as mean as his an' was threatenin' to go public with how Jonesie'd cheated on her every chance he got. So he'd hopped onto Claussen's bandwagon. He had an article comin' out in one of the sports weeklies, an' Donna couldn't help but listen as Ivan told me how Bush'd talked with Barrow 'bout the whole episode an' was threatenin' some major new revelations. Like enough shit hadn't been said, already. Ivan kept assurin' me he had nothin' to back up his claims, but now Donna was as nervous as me, looked like, the way she kept movin' about. Then Weiss showed up, said some casual stuff 'bout how easy things were gonna be an' lead us to the studio.

It was a nice set-up – comfy chair for him to sit in, a nice couch for me an' Donna, a small table in front with glasses of water for us. Lights were soft an' warm. It's funny, but lookin' at that set made me more sure I could trust Doug Weiss than anything else could of.

We sat down an' Weiss sat before us as the technicians attached our mikes, an' he kept askin' us if we're comfortable. Well, I was as comfortable as I could be facin' down the lions in a suit that was already a good size too small. I couldn't button anything on it without bulgin' over, so my collar was undone an' I had no tie on. I was wishin' to God I'd gone ahead an' bought a new one in Tahoe, like Donna. She was wearin' this light flowin' dress that just sort of drifted around her in a green haze. She looked so beautiful in it, it hurt, an' it helped make her seem real cool an' calm, once we were set. Only thing she said was, "I may need a couple of breaks, this kid is already so big. I think he'll be taking after Bobby's side of the family."

Weiss smiled an' was all, "This shouldn't take long. The segment will probably be about ten minutes, and we have half an hour to shoot it,

so if you need a break, just say so. And keep in mind, Bobby, Donna –
there are a lot of people out there rooting for you to get past this trauma.
Just tell the truth and everything should work out fine."

I nodded, took a sip of water, an' we got down to business.

SHOW TRANSCRIPT 08/20

WEISS: Welcome back to "Weiss on Sports." Now many of you may recall, a few months back, Bobby Carapisi, one of the Golden State Griffins' best relief pitchers, was kidnapped and brutally assaulted by a group of men in West Los Angeles. He wound up hospitalized for several days with serious injuries and was kept on the DL for a total of forty-five days. To his everlasting credit, Bobby's worked his way back into the bullpen and has even closed a couple of close road games, almost saving one and just missing with the other. Unfortunately, during his recuperation a great many unfounded rumors began swirling about in regards to Bobby's attack. He took the high road in an attempt to let them just drift away, but instead the rumors and half-truths have only multiplied and intensified, thanks to the web-blogs and scandal sheets. So now Bobby has joined me, accompanied by his wife, Donna, to try and clarify the events of that night and get everything out in the open. Bobby, Donna, thank you for joining me.

BOBBY: Glad to, Doug.

DONNA: Thank you for having us.

WEISS: Let's get right down to business. Tell us in your own words what happened on that horrible night in June.

BOBBY: I don't know what happened, that's the thing. I went to the store for my wife, y'know, and as I was getting in my car, somebody hit me from behind. I know they yanked me in the back of a truck...a van...and hit me, some more, and I remember thinking I hope they don't kill me, but the rest is blurry, just quick flashes of things, y'know...like I'm fading in and out of awareness. Next thing I really know is, I'm in the hospital.

WEISS: Did you get a look at the men who hit you?

BOBBY: No. I heard somebody say something, then as I was turning, that's when I got hit.

WEISS: Some claimed the doctor's report said all you had were some cuts, bruises and two cracked ribs. A number of people have wondered why they kept you in the hospital for so long over what they are considered relatively minor injuries.

BOBBY: It...it was more than that. I mean – .

DONNA: He also had a severe concussion. And he kept passing out on us. He'd be in the middle of a conversation with someone then just drift into silence, and the next thing you know, he's unconscious.

WEISS: That must have been pretty frightening.

DONNA: It was.

WEISS: Did the doctors find out what was happening?

DONNA: They ran a huge battery of tests...

BOBBY: Holy Mary, so many.

DONNA: They had to. He scored ten on the Glasgow Coma Scale.

WEISS: Glasgow Coma Scale?

DONNA: It's a test the paramedics use to find out if there's been head trauma. The ER doctor explained it to me. Told me Bobby'd been found wandering around, babbling. His head was covered in blood. It took them several minutes to calm him down enough just to treat him let alone bring him to the hospital.

WEISS: Sounds terrifying.

DONNA: It was. And that's on top of me already being crazy with worry.

WEISS: How long was he missing?

DONNA: More than six hours after that woman called police.

WEISS: Do you think he was just wandering about for that long?

DONNA: Possibly. I was told some cuts had begun to clot.

WEISS: And you don't have any idea where you were, Bobby? All that time?

BOBBY: Like I said, y'know, I...I don't remember any of it. One of the paramedics come by my room later...and he told me I was more worried about losing my car than about all the blood I'd lost.

DONNA: He lost a great deal. The paramedics said his skin was pasty where it was visible. And Bobby's olive-skinned and always looks...he always looked so very healthy.

WEISS: So what about the blackouts? Did they find a cause for them?

DONNA: Well...initially, doctors were afraid he might have a brain stem injury, but the final conclusion was, it was probably related to a couple of bruises they found...on the left frontal area of his cerebrum... and...and in the back area, hear the stem.

WEISS: That sounds serious.

DONNA: Yes. Yes.

BOBBY: But...but the bruising's pretty much gone, now, and my ribs are healed good. Fact, I'm heading out with the team on a road trip, tomorrow, in case they need me in the bullpen.

WEISS: Yes, The Griffins' bullpen has become pretty lean.

BOBBY: But, y'know, I gotta say, The Griffns've been great. They've really backed me up. Stood behind me, all the way. Fantastic bunch of guys. Tanner. Starsky. Rizal. I dunno how I'd of got through this without them all.

WEISS: Glad to hear it. So have you gotten any word from the police as to how their investigation's going?

BOBBY: It's being handled by the sheriff's department, and they don't have much to go on, y'know. I didn't see the guys what hit me. The store surveillance tapes don't show much. I dunno if they'll ever find them.

WEISS: What about this man...William Barrow...who you supposedly picked out of a police lineup?

BOBBY: It was from a bunch of pictures they showed me, and I...I thought recognized him. But then I got to thinking...I think I picked him out just because I saw him in the store. Just before it happened. We even talked a little at the register. He probably didn't have nothing to do with it.

WEISS: There's another young man who claims otherwise.

BOBBY: Yeah. That waiter.

WEISS: Eric Larson.

BOBBY: Yeah.

WEISS: Did you read last Sunday's article in the Times?

BOBBY: Yeah, I did.

DONNA: It really upset him. I don't know what really happened between this...this Larson person and that man, William Barrow, if anything.

WEISS: You read the article?

DONNA: Yes.

BOBBY: You did?!

DONNA: While you were out running.

BOBBY: Donna, I asked you – .

DONNA: I know, I know. But I had to know exactly what was in the article, and it sounds to me like those men – Larson and Barrow – have different versions of what happened. Completely opposite versions.

WEISS: So, Bobby, what Larson claims was done to him, that was not done to you?

BOBBY: No.

WEISS: How can you be so sure?

BOBBY: What?

WEISS: You said you were out of it, from the time you were hit to when you reached the hospital. How can you be sure?

BOBBY: Well...I...y'know, I think I'd...if somebody did to me what was done to him, I think I'd know it, know what I mean.

DONNA: Don't forget – Bobby was severely beaten. Eric Larson wasn't. And he had so little evidence to back up his claims, the District Attorney refused to even consider pressing charges.

WEISS: True. So why do you think Larson claimed his assault and yours were committed by the same man?

DONNA: If he was assaulted.

WEISS: That's another good point.

BOBBY: Look, I don't know why he's doing this. I never even met the guy. Don't know what he looks like. Anything. But what's in the paper's enough for me to think, I don't know, maybe he's after the guy for money. People do that in this town.

WEISS: Ain't that the truth?

BOBBY: All I know is, what he says happened to him didn't happen to me. I don't care what anybody claims.

WEISS: What about William Barrow's new claims?

BOBBY: Like what?

WEISS: He's apparently saying you and he had consensual relations in – .

BOBBY: I'm not gay. Okay?

WEISS: Nobody's saying you are, but – .

BOBBY: Look, I got nothing against gay people. My favorite uncle was gay. He was also the coolest dude in all of Philly. I met other people who're gay and I got no problem with any of 'em. You leave me alone, I'm fine with you.

WEISS: You know, it sounds like you're familiar with Barrow's new claim.

BOBBY: Yeah. One of the cops investigating what happened told me what he said. First, the guy says he's got nothing to do with anything. Then he's got me in his car an' we're having fun because I'm so hard up, I got to get some relief and I don't care from who. I mean, look at me. Do I look like the kind of guy who's into that? Has anybody even suggested something like that about me, before?

WEISS: Not that I've been able to find.

BOBBY: Yeah. Well. Not that anybody's been able to find. With a guy or a girl. And that includes those...those reporters who're after my...after me on it.

WEISS: Claussen, Bush and Langston. They have taken a real dislike to you.

BOBBY: Yeah, well, Himori told me all about their work.

WEISS: That'd be Toshiro Himori, who heads the team's press office.

BOBBY: Yeah. He says Claussen's a freak on gays in baseball. Hates even the thought of it. Couple years back, when some manager said he thought baseball'd be open to having a gay guy on a team, he went nuts trying to figure out who it was that manager was talking about, even though the guy'd said he wasn't referring to anybody, in particular. Claussen went so far as to accuse this one shortstop of being the one then had to back down when the guy sued him.

WEISS: Freddy Bowen, I remember that. Although, he didn't actually sue Claussen; he just threatened to.

BOBBY: He still backed down.

WEISS: True.

DONNA: He was probably afraid someone would notice how loud he was being about it and start looking into his own background.

WEISS: What do you mean, Donna?

DONNA: Oh, to paraphrase Shakespeare: "The gentleman doth protest too much, methinks."

WEISS: Well...Donna...

BOBBY: Yeah, that's my wife. She's got a degree in English.

DONNA: And I'm working on my Master's.

WEISS: That's great. What play was that quote from?

DONNA: "Hamlet."

WEISS: And what exactly did you mean by it?

DONNA: Well there must be some reason for these men to spread their lies. Bobby's done nothing to them. He was the victim of a brutal unwarranted attack and they're trying to twist it into something vile and scandalous, and I have to wonder why. I have to wonder what their agenda is. Because they aren't just aiming their cruelty toward my husband, they're also aiming it at me and my children.

WEISS: In all fairness, I don't think any of these men means to hurt you or – .

DONNA: Anything they say about Bobby affects us. Any lies they spread about him are lies about us. I don't care what they claim their reasons are, any attack on Bobby is an attack on his entire family.

And I have to wonder why those men would be so cruel as to deliberately hurt a four-year-old child just because they don't like her father.

WEISS: Uh...well, I suppose that's a valid question, Donna. And I wonder if any of the men you're referring to are capable of answering it.

DONNA: If they haven't the nerve to answer me, let them tell my daughter. She's begun to ask me why those bad men are trying to hurt daddy.

WEISS: She knows what's going on?

DONNA: How can she not? I've had reporters appear at my front door, with my child in my hands, asking me about things that are too disgusting to even think about. And not caring that my daughter is hearing it.

BOBBY: And that really pisses me off. Oops, can I say that on T-V?

WEISS: Why not? They use it in Primetime all the time.

BOBBY: Okay, well, you want to come after me, that's fine. But do it like a man. Face to face. Not like some rat hiding in the shadows till my back's turned then go after my wife and kid.

WEISS: I doubt that'll happen. Well, we're almost out of time. Anything else to add, Bobby?

BOBBY: All I got left to say is, I got a wife I love. I got a daughter I'd die for. I got a son on the way. And Donna and me, we want to have more.

DONNA: We both come from large families.

BOBBY: And I love doing what I do for a living. How anybody could...anybody could think I'd jeopardize all that for...I mean, for...well, over something I could...well, I wouldn't need to go to anybody else for, know what I mean?

WEISS: I think we get the picture.

BOBBY: How they think I could throw all that away for nothing is beyond me. I don't know what else I can say. I really don't.

WEISS: Nor do I. Bobby, Donna, thanks again for being on the show.

BOBBY: I appreciate you having us, Doug.

WEISS: And good luck with everything.

DONNA: Yes.

WEISS: And there you have it. Bobby and Donna Carapisi, trying to set the record straight. And I have to add, after talking with this fine young couple, I now wonder myself exactly why anyone would push the idea that Bobby's anything but a normal decent young man who loves his family as much as he loves playing baseball. I can only reiterate what I've said before: this looks even more like a case of mistaken identity, where a young man, who was in the wrong place at the wrong time, was attacked by a group of thugs who, if they'd realized who he was, might have asked him to autograph their baseball bat instead of hit him with it. Such occurrences have become all too common in Los Angeles, as of late, probably because of the reticence by our law enforcement officials to actually enforce anti-hate statutes. To my mind, serious questions should be raised about the conduct and attitudes of the LA County Sheriff's deputies and District Attorney's office, who seem far more interested in letting this case die quietly than in solving it. And why anyone in the sports reporting world would go after Bobby Carapisi over this is simply beyond me...unless Donna's query is on the money – that they have a hidden agenda and are trying to deflect attention from their own peccadilloes. But that would be a whole 'nother story. Back in a moment with the wrap up of today's show.

<u>END OF TRANSCRIPT</u>

I gotta say, I felt good about things after that show aired. Weiss told me from the start it was a good one, but I figured he was just yappin'. But then Ivan an' Himori both called me to say I'd done good an' Donna was a perfect back-up for me. In every way. Plus Himori'd got hold of Claussen's article an' it looked like I may of cut its impact in half. He wouldn't tell me what's in it, just said it was a hatchet job. So I went online to check it out, myself.

Man...I dunno what I did to Claussen, but he had me down as a faggot. Period. No holds barred. Made fun of the way I walked an' talked an' held my bat, like I was a... was some...wait – what's the phrase he used? Queen from Jersey – an' he made a big deal of how I'm just havin' my second kid when I'm supposed to be this big Italian-Catholic stud an' when most guys my age married long as I was already had three or four. Never mind how Tony's still without kids an' Mary Elizabeth's just about to have her first, after years of tryin'. But that was just the lead-in for his interview with that Barrow guy.

The skinny little fuck changed his story, again. Yeah, he still claimed he'd picked me up, but now it was more like a seduction. Like he "talked me into it. I know it's wrong, but he was so beautiful and I could tell he was open to it." So I got in his car an' he drove me to a secluded spot in Beverly Hills an' he...he sucked me off. Then – here's where the story really gets crazy-weird – this Larson guy showed up with a baseball bat an' started hittin' us with it, screamin' he was gonna kill him. I just got caught in the middle of it all. Holy Mary, he made it sound so...so simple an' logical. An' people were readin' that shit like it was absolute truth.

Problem with Barrow's story was, Claussen was in such a rush to get the story out, he didn't check with Larson. An' the guy wasn't even in town, that day. He was in Vegas. Had proof. An' he showed it to everybody. Man, he ripped Claussen a new one. On the news. In the papers. He mouthed off left an' right on how dumb the story was. I didn't have to say a word except, "That guy, Barrow's a liar." It was diamonds.

Now Bush...Bush just flat out said I was the one lyin'. He started off from his own stories 'bout me steppin' out on Donna then mixed in Barrow's crap with Roscoe's ideas to paint me as some kind of – shit, what was the phrase Claussen used? – oh, "stealth homo" tryin' to infiltrate the sacred game of baseball an' push through some agenda to make the game open to men who'd just love to share a shower with real men like Lorraine an' Verdugo an' stuff. Fact, he even got Lorraine to say one reason he hadn't minded bein' traded was how I kept lookin' at him the locker room as he dressed an' makin' comments that said I wanted him. Yap, yap, yap. Fuckin' asshole. That's the reason he was traded – nobody could stand his crap, anymore. He's always had this attitude of, I'm hot shit an' you're chicken shit. I heard he's about to get traded from Cincie 'cause the players there hate his guts, too. Not that I care 'bout that fuckin' team, but it's proof how you can't take anybody's comments for real.

But then in his Friday column, first one after the show, Bush interviewed this guy in San Fran who said he'd given me some head, too. Named dates an' went on an' on 'bout how the last time we'd done it, back in May. After the game. How I'd come over his place an' we'd gone...we went farther than ever before. Meanin' I...I'd done him. An' he said it was love. Made me sick.

But what made it perfect was, Bush pulled a boner. He didn't check to make sure the game got played. An' it didn't. It was called on account of rain an' rescheduled since we were off to Colorado the next day. We hadn't even stayed in town but left early. Weiss jumped him on that one, as did some guys from the cable networks. "Stupid to be taken in by a publicity-seeking homosexual."

So there I was, two for two in my favor. Both the main assholes goin' after me looked like idiots, an' Langston was keepin' quiet. If only it'd ended there. But it didn't.

"COLLISION"

I got a call from Pete, the reporter I'd spoken with, that Monday morning. I was still pissed at him for how the article made me sound, so I didn't answer my cell when I saw who it was. He left a message. When I heard it, I called him back. He started off by trying to explain, but I cut in.

"You said you had more info about Allen, Pete," I snapped. "Just tell me what you're talking about."

"Bobby Carapisi was on Doug Weiss' show, last night, and he's swearing that – a) he was not sexually assaulted; b) he really was mistaken about Allen Barrow and c) he thinks you're just using the situation to make some money." Any hint of niceness was gone from his tone. "Now my editors want to know something. How much of a liar ARE you?"

If that was meant to startle me into a confession or something, he was a little late. I'd already been slammed by Grant. Before the paper even hit the streets he called, and he was not happy. In fact, he was screaming. "What've you done!? What the hell've you done!?"

"Given that bitch ADA – ."

Nor was he listening. "You fucking idiot! All you've done is make life hell for a man who may not've even been involved! I've got two Sheriff's detectives screaming at me that I've fucked up their investigation and – ."

"WHAT fucking investigation?! They weren't doing ANYthing! They were gonna let it just go away!"

" – and Ionescue's on my ass, along with the fucking DA! They think I set you up for this!"

"Fuck her!" I screamed back. "And fuck you and fuck the DA and fuck the fucking sheriff's department! He fucking raped me! Up my ass and in my mouth! And I gave you everything you needed to arrest that son-of-a-bitch, and you didn't do a goddamn thing! Well, I've put mother-fucking Allen Barrow on notice! I let him know he pulls this shit, again, his ass is in jail! Him and his fucking friends! And that's more than you fucking did!"

And I hung up. Well...disconnected the call. Then remembered I was in the middle of a Carl's Junior Burger. A packed Carl's Junior Burger. And the place was...oh, suddenly very quiet. With everyone looking at me. And the manager on his way over. I mustered as much dignity as I could, gathered my meal and headed for my car, only half caring that I'd just scarred a dozen children for life. At least, if you could believe the eyes of their mothers and fathers.

Of course, Ionescue called, too, but the second I heard, "Eric, this is Beth and I'm very disappointed in – ," I hung up on her and turned my cell phone off so I could collect my thoughts. And, to be honest, revel in the impact I was finally having. Preen over the idea that I was ruffling a few official feathers and making more than one person wish to God they'd never ignored me.

That was on a Friday. Before I'd read the article. When I finally did, my mood spun into a downward spiral. Yeah, Pete carped about how I was treated and compared it to how Bobby was protected, but by the end of the vile thing, it was all just a misunderstanding on St. Bobby's part as regards Allen, and the police and system of justice were screwed up, and me? This is a big one – I came out looking like your two-bit whore who was trying to make a buck off someone else's tragedy. Oh, sure, he paid lip service to my assault but in his best "even-handed" manner just had to point out that there were serious questions about what had happened. Which no one had any real answers to. So he let Allen's comments about me stand. And not even stand untouched. No, they were all but presented as the perfect suggestion as to what might really have happened, even if he didn't really want to say so. I felt like I'd been gutted like a carp Gramma'd hooked while out ice fishing.

Then I started getting calls from all sorts of people – reporters asking for quotes on a follow-up article, talk show hosts wondering if I'd be available to bare my soul this Tuesday for a Thursday afternoon broadcast, religious fanatics telling me I'd be fine if I'd just turn my life over to Jesus or simply to bitch me out for being a queer, sports freaks pissed I'd mixed "Mr. Delivery" up in a faggot sex ring, yada, yada, yada; how they got my cell phone number, I don't know. I had to turn it off and unplug my landline, but that only shifted people to sending spam to my Hotmail account till I set it on "don't accept anything from anybody I don't know".

It's weird, but not once during this period – and I'm talking about from the time I received the tape to when the article was published – did I think about working. So I didn't make a dime. And then I couldn't, since I never knew which call would be a client and which would be someone telling me I'll burn in hell, and I just couldn't handle the overflow of acid being sloshed my way. But then a look at my vanishing bank account convinced me I'd better just live with it and hope I could make a few bucks, soon. So I turned my phone back on and faked being the wrong number, once I figured out who it was.

The next day is when Pete called, pretending what he'd written was all well and good, and basically asking if I was credible in any way, form or fashion.

"What the fuck do you care?" I answered. "You're convinced I'm just this whore junky who's not worth anybody's time – ."

"Are you?"

A week earlier, that would have sent me on a screaming fit. Now? I just sighed. "Does it matter? People already have their minds made up and nobody's doing a damn thing about it. Not you. Not the cops. Not anybody. Nobody fucking cares. They just want it to go away, so all they're going to do is beat up on the queer who was fucked and let the queer-fucker walk. Thank you so much for making it easier for them."

He must have wanted me to scream and cuss, or something, because his voice changed. Grew softer.

"Eric, you have to understand. What I heard was three completely different, but also completely plausible, versions of an occurrence."

"And as Pilate said, 'What is truth?' Right."

"Eric..."

"I know, I know," I sneered. "It's just all so very 'Rashomon'."

"What's that?"

"Nothing. Old Japanese movie."

"You like old movies?" He seemed incredulous.

"My mom likes 'em. And we'd watch 'em, together." Great way to spend a snow day...or days, in Minnesota. Build up the Netflix pile and OD on Humphrey Bogart, Cary Grant, William Holden. Fellini. Renoir. Truffaut. Kurosawa. Bergman. I added, "I grew up wanting to be Burt Lancaster, not Tom Cruise or Hanks or any other Tom. Once upon a time. Now...?"

"Sounds like you've given up on the acting."

"C'mon, Pete, who'd hire me? Only movie I could get on now is porno. Maybe some of the gay shit that's on 'Here!', but that's it. That's over."

"You were really serious about an acting career?"

I didn't register the subtext, at that moment – "You mean you weren't lying about that, too?" I just shrugged.

"Yeah, but maybe I was just fooling myself. I wouldn't be the first to do that. Hell, I won't be the last."

"Yeah. Right."

"So...what else did he say about me?"

"Who?"

"The guy – shit, uh, Bobby. On that show."

"Haven't you seen it?

"I didn't even know about it till you told me."

He hesitated. "Would you like to?"

I was surprised. "Why?"

"To see for yourself what he's saying. There's been too much second-hand and third-person info shifting around here. I have a download of the program. You can come down to the office. Watch it on my computer."

I went. Still don't know why, but I did. I sat at Pete's way too neat desk and watched the whole interview on his oversized monitor. As he watched me. And for the first time, I saw Bobby. Saw him fight for his life. Saw him all but beg everyone to let this thing go and leave him alone. His outward manner was basically calm and cool, but on several occasions, his eyes flashed with fear and pain. And I knew what for.

It HAD happened to him, just like it had to me. And he was barely hanging on. And his wife was offering him nothing in the way of a lifeline. On several occasions, he took her hand; not once did she take his. He'd put his arm around her; she wouldn't lean in to it or even react. She'd worn a dress that would emphasize her pregnancy and her taste in clothes; but he was in a suit that didn't fit and made him look...well, big and stupid, for want of better words. And despite all the things they said about each other – all the things she said to back him up – it was obvious the love in that relationship was uni-directional. And for the first time I got a glimmer of the idea that I had done something horribly, horribly wrong.

When it was done, I sat there. Pete didn't say a word, just let me be. And the only thought I was really aware of just kept repeating itself in my warped little mind – "What have I done? What have I done? What have I done?" Finally, I turned to him and said, "Believe him."

"And not you?" I shook my head. "Why?"

"Look at him," I said, and went for a lie that anyone could accept as truth. "He's big, he's straight; not like me."

"Are you sure?"

"No question," and on that I was NOT lying. I could tell Bobby had zero interest in men, sexually. Call it gay-dar if you want, but the reality is, looking at him and how he acted and all that jazz, he was obviously as heterosexual as I was gay. "Totally straight. And as much as I hate Allen for what he did to me, I cannot see him picking this guy to do it to. I got the feeling they liked guys who were slim, not bear-sized like Bobby."

"He's put on some weight."

I rolled my eyes and went to IMDb.com to pull up the only picture of me on there. It was from my one great moment in a sit-com, standing next to the lead actress. The clothes were tight, so Pete could see I was never anywhere near what you'd call beefy. He nodded.

"Yeah. When Carapisi was attacked, he weighed a good forty pounds more than you. But it could've just been a crime of opportunity."

I shook my head. "Allen and his buddies planned my attack. They don't go looking for chance victims. They search for what they think will be fun, plan it out and then take it. I think you jumped the gun on making Bobby part of this." I had to have at least one dig back at him for that brutal story.

"Me!?"

"I didn't bring him into this. I didn't know anything about him."

"Okay, okay. Maybe. Just maybe. But I'm gonna look into it, some more."

"Pete, seriously, believe him."

We left it at that. I hoped he would follow my advice and let the poor guy alone. I felt bad enough about what I'd started. No need to add to it.

I was glad I left Pete on better terms. Because a few days later, a story came out declaring I was the one who'd beaten Bobby up. Talk about out of left field, to use what I think is a baseball analogy. It was some anti-gay sports reporter who never even tried to verify his story with me. I guess he figured some faggot-whore wouldn't be able – or willing – to fight back. But when I heard about it from Rusty (he had to sneak a call to me because Laila was still pissed about me dissing her at Rene's) I got a copy of the rag and read it. Problem is, I was in Las Vegas with a client, that day. I'd even won at roulette (always bet on black) and had kept the receipt for taxes. I contacted Pete, gave him a copy of it and he fired back. Big-time. It was magnificent.

But then the tabloids hit. I saw them while standing in line at the Von's near me. Not the big splashy headlines, at first; just banners 'cross the tops – "Bobby Carapisi Admits He's Queer!" and "Bobby C Tells Wife He's Gay!" I almost didn't notice them, but a woman ahead of me shoved one back into the wrong slot and it fell out and all but jumped up at me.

I bought them and read them both, and they were slaughter jobs. One had telephoto pictures of Bobby slapping Donna and looking like a total beast. And below them, a photo of Allen with the caption, "I picked him up as he was picking out bananas." The story was totally Allen's version, right down to them both being gay-bashed. The other presented the same basic story, but I guess they weren't willing to pay big bucks for the physical photos and Allen's story, because all they had was Bobby leaning against the deck railing, back to the camera as Donna screamed at him. It looked like he was completely non-challant, and they made it seem as if Bobby was coming out of the closet to his wife and she wasn't taking it well.

I felt cold as I read them. Icy to my toes. And I knew – deep down I knew – this was never going to just go away. Not now. The sharks smelled blood and, Jesus God, I'd put it there. And I had no idea how to stop it.

While the sports creeps dropped the volume on me, all of a sudden these guys from some gay groups started usin' the uproar to back up their ideas about "homophobia in professional sports." Me not bein' gay didn't matter; they figured I was an' I "had" to stay in the closet an' force myself to keep a wife 'cause if I didn't, I'd get dropped from the roster an' nobody'd hire me. To them, me swearin' I was straight was proof I was really queer, like that makes sense.

But, man...it got to where, no matter where I went, reporters found me an' wanted to talk to me an' photographers wanted to snap my picture. All in the space of a couple days! But even then, I'm thinkin', once I get back to playin' an' show 'em I still got it, everything'll die down. So I stayed nice. Fuckin' bit my tongue a couple times to do it, too.

Donna...she stayed home, most days. Aunt T started comin' over to keep her company an' bring stuff in. We tried one of those online orderin' services for groceries, but the guy drivin' the truck got paid a ton to let 'em see what big-bad-Bobby was eatin'. It was sick. Still, I played along. Just let it go, Bobby, let it go.

I didn't realize how bad it was till we were at Dallas, but then... aw, shit, I guess everybody knows that by now. The sports creeps made plenty out of it.

It was the second of a three-game patch, an' we'd beat 'em in the first one. Morgan was on the mound; their big guy, Lazz – Zelazney, was at bat, which wasn't good. Morgan'd walked one guy an' come close to losin' a dinger off the second, an' Lazz was one of Dallas' power hitters. We were up by two an' it was bottom of the seventh. Rizal'd wanted to pull Morgan before he'd hit the mound but Starsky'd overruled him. Now he was havin' second thoughts, 'cause he had me warmin' up in the bullpen.

I was feelin' okay...I guess. I mean, I got strikes off Lazz before, but he's also copped a couple base hits off me. Still I figured I could at least make a good show. Even if I kept him to a single I could of stranded him at first – I knew I'd have no trouble gettin' the next two guys out. It'd look okay.

But there was this guy. This asshole in the stands next the bullpen. He recognized me.

Now this was on a Friday afternoon. Been a week since the supermarket rags'd hit the stands, all over the country, an' those ones claimin' I told my wife I'm gay was already part of the sports chatter. "You heard this story 'bout Bobby C?" "Can you believe that shit?" "C'mon, it's a scandal rag; how much can you believe that crap?" "But it's not just them." "You mean, he really is gay?" "Cut it out; he's got a wife an' about to have his second kid." "This blows holes in that story he told, 'bout being attacked." "I hear some guys are into being hurt." "That's sick." Yap, yap, yap. But I could already see signs it was gonna blow over an' I had my new contract, so I was gonna be cool about it.

Yeah, that's me – cool all over. Calm as a cloud in the sky. Sure people were already razzin' me from the stands. Home teams're always the worst, but that's part of the game, y'know. You get to where you don't really hear 'em; they're just this buzz in the background, like a fly or a gnat, an' you ignore it 'cause you got a job to do. Just don't listen...don't pay attention. Not till they make you.

An' that asshole in Dallas...he got me first.

Now I'm in the pen, just lobbin' balls over to Jay. Hadn't even really started up the serious stuff, yet. An' this asshole behind me, he's already yellin' out, "Shit, he even throws like faggot," an' "Hey, Bobby, my grandmother throws balls harder'n that," an' shit. Now, I got my focus on. I mean, I can hear him, but he's nothin' to me. No big deal. But he's pissin' off Jay.

I could see it, so I just popped off with, "C'mon, Jay, fuck him. He's just an asshole."

The asshole hears me an' say, "Yeah, you'd LIKE to fuck me, wouldn't you, faggot? Or maybe just suck on this?"

That's when Jay loses it and screams, "You fuck! You sick fuckin' bastard!"

I looked 'round...an' he's got this banana stickin' out his fly! An' he's wavin' it at me, laughin'. An' there's this boy sittin' right by him! Maybe seven, eight years old! An' he's laughin', too! That's when I lost it.

"You do that 'round your kid?! What kind of sick freak are you?!"

"Hey, you don't fuckin' talk to me 'bout my kid, cocksucker!"

Then he threw the banana at me. Hit me in the face. I didn't even think. I grabbed it back up and slung it back at him. Hit him dead in the eye. He screamed and fell back, an' his kid started screamin', an' what Jay told me later was, I was screamin'. Trying to climb the fence to get to the bastard. It took him, Starsky an' Rizal to keep me from gettin' up to him.

Well...I got tossed. Threatened with suspension. But the good thing was, one of the cameras caught the guy an' me havin' it out. Caught him throwin' the banana an' even caught a little of his language. So when he filed assault against me, Himori made me file assault charges right back at him. They all got dropped. The asshole still got a lawyer, but last I heard, that was goin' nowhere. Might get dropped, too. Himori got me a great pit-bull to shout back at him.

But that wasn't it. That wasn't the end. No. That came in Cincinnati, a week later. Coach put me back in rotation an' I was ready to do anything to make him happy with me. So when it began lookin' good for me to go out, I was ready. An' I swore to God nobody...fuckin' nobody was gonna get to me, this time.

It was bottom of the eighth. We were up by one. Morgan walked the first guy – Portillo? Second up got a base hit, so there's a man on first and second. Then he was down to a two-two count an' their pitcher, Scott, was at bat. An' he was tryin'. He got six fouls in a row off Morgan before Rizal sent me in. Not the best situation to relieve, but all I needed to do was get one more strike with Scott. Shouldn't be too hard; he loves fast balls...so he's sure I won't toss him one, so maybe I will. Maybe he'll lose it an' swing, an' pop one up for Wash or Petre to catch. Make it easy on me.

I did more warmin' up from the mound. Coleman was catchin' an' it was just like old times. I got so focused on followin' his lead, I couldn't hear the people who were callin' my name. I mean, it sounded like the usual chant – "Bob-beee...Bob-beeee...Bobby Cara-peeeseee." That's supposed to cut your concentration, but this time? Never even slowed me down.

Once I was ready, Coleman called a time out an' come up to the mound to hand me the ball. An' he's all, "I watched him his last up. He'll go for any fastball, but he's spooked by sliders. Morgan wouldn't do one, so let's try those on him." Normally I'd of argued, but this time I just nodded. He soft-punched me on the shoulder, somethin' he never did, an' said, "You'll be okay, kid."

I made myself grin at him then he trotted back.

The noise level was gettin' deafer, like a dull roar, all in unison. But I was ready for it. I got set for the pitch. An' wound up. An' Scott hunkered down. An' Coleman was set. An' the chant kept growin'. Like half the stadium was fuckin' screamin' it.

"Bob-beee...Bob-beee...Bobby Car-ra-peesee!"

I still wasn't hearin' it. I let loose the pitch in a slider...an' Scott almost went for it. Almost. He had to check his bat to keep from tryin' for it. Whoa...so fuckin' close to a strike. So fuckin' close. But now he was wary of me, so Coleman signaled for a fastball. I nodded.

The roar was gettin' louder. I was too used to the crap. Shut it out. Shut him down. That's all that matters, baby. I wound up. Got ready to let her fly...an' Scott got it first. He stepped out of position just as I let the ball go. Man, it would've been a perfect strike.

I was pretty ticked off, but Coleman was spittin' nails. He shot up from his crouch, callin' on the ump to call it a strike for what Scott pulled, but the ump wasn't havin' it an' Scott wasn't listenin'. He was lookin' 'round the stands, his jaw open in disbelief. They were his fans, in his team's hometown, an' he was all shook up from what he was hearin'.

Coleman caught it, next. So did most the other players on the field. Even the guys in the dugout caught it. Guess I was the last to understand what they were sayin'. I mean, it still sounded like my name...but it didn't, know what I'm sayin'. It's like, what WERE they sayin'? Wasn't my name.

But then somethin' got tossed on the field. Somethin' long an' yellow. A fuckin' banana. There we were on national T-V with thousands of fans callin' the same thing, over an' over an' over. "Bob-beee...Bob-beee..." An' they're tossin' bananas an' crap on the field. An' then it hits me like a chunk of ice in the face what they're sayin': "Bobby's ass is eeeasee!"

Crap started rainin' down, then. Holy Mary, did it. Papers an' bananas an' what looked like sausages, none of it gettin' close to me but makin' for a lot of hell on the guys near the stands. An' I just froze there. Just froze. 'Cause all of it brought this...this...this screamin' nightmare of a memory. Of the first guy on top me. Slammin' into my brain, ridin' those words like you'd ride a wave.

"Bobby-Bobby-Bobby's ass is easy!" FUCK!

It was this...this roar...this wall of sound crashin' over me...an' more crashed in with it. Shrieked in with it. The second guy. The last guy. That skinny little fuck. The punches an' the slaps an' the hands an' the blood an' on top it all's this squeal of a knife twistin' in my heart.

"Bobby, Bobby, Bobby's ass is easy!"

I...I couldn't think. I couldn't speak. I just listened to the crowd snarlin' at me, over an' over, louder an' louder. I remember Scott gesturin' at the stands, pissed, but I couldn't hear him. I remember Starsky an' Chief stormin' over to the home base umpire, red in the face, screamin' at the top of their lungs...but I couldn't hear them, either. The loud speakers began squawkin' like the announcer was tryin' to say somethin', trying to shout over the crowd...but I couldn't hear him, either. It's like the only words I could understand were those six god-awful things the crowd was chantin'.

"Bobby. Bobby. Bobby's ass is easy."

They were like razor blades slicin' at my eyes an' brain. My gut threatened to make things worse by havin' me lose my lunch right there in front of God an' everybody. My head felt like I was about to take off or somethin'. Then I noticed Lorraine in Cincie's dugout, smirkin' at me. He blew me a kiss an'...an' that motherfucker...asshole that he was, he centered me. I wasn't gonna give int' their shit without tryin' to back up my team. I couldn't let the guys down. I couldn't. I couldn't. I couldn't.

So I made myself get back into stance, holdin' the ball ready for a pitch. But Coleman didn't move. He was lookin' at me with this... this confused expression, like he was tryin' to figure out why they were sayin' what they were sayin' 'bout me...or maybe wonderin' if it was true. Whatever it was, he didn't move. Then Scott started yellin' at him an' gesturin' for him to squat as he took his position. Coleman still didn't move. I screamed at him, "Lemme pitch to him, you son-of-a-bitch, Holy Mary, lemme pitch to him!" I knew Scott'd take the strike an' then it'd be okay for me to leave the field an' them bring another reliever on for the next batter.

Tears were streamin' down my face as I held the ball an' waited for Coleman to get into position...an' the God-damn-mother-fuckin'-son-of-a-bitch wouldn't move. He wouldn't move. He wouldn't fuckin' move.

The roar kept growin' an' the pain kept buildin' an' I started to see nothin' but black...this deep, blindin', empty, terrifyin' black. An' everything I'd ever remembered about that...that night kept slammin' back into me, an' I could feel it...all of it. I could feel it.

I could taste it.

I could smell it.

I couldn't stop it.

I couldn't stop it.

An' the ball dropped from my hand. An' I...I don't know when it happened, but I was on my knees, lookin' at the ground an' shakin' out of control.

Rizal an' Scott come over, lifted me to my feet an' guided me away. They lead me back to the dugout, past all the guys. Even Coleman, who couldn't look at me, no more. An' the whole way, Scott's tellin' me, "They're assholes, Bobby, they're motherfuckin' assholes. Don't listen to 'em, Bobby; they're assholes." Then Starsky took over from him an' they took me into the lockers. An' every step of the way it followed me. Echoed down the hall. Drove itself into my brain like needles. Over an' over an' over.

"Bobby. Bobby. Bobby's ass is easy."

"POLITICS AND COMMENTARY TODAY"

TRANSCRIPT FOR SHOW #091108

Host: Clifford Morrison

Guests: Dr. Vera Blumenthal

Ian Dekka

Rahim Condury

Eric Larson

Nicholas O'Crohan

[Audience applause]

CLIFF: That's right. So, good morning and welcome to the Monday edition of "Politics and Commentary Today". Our guests for today's program are Dr. Vera Blumenthal, head of Human Sciences at U.C.C. and author of, "Humanity Is More Than Just Being Human." Quite a mouthful, that.

VERA: But it says it all.

CLIFF: Must be a textbook. Thank you for coming. Also, we have Nicholas O'Crohan, managing editor of "Sports Today Magazine."

NICK: Cliff.

[Audience applause]

CLIFF: Pleasure to have you, again. Ian Dekka, founder of "The Gay Alliance For Equality Rights" and columnist for "Stonewall Continues," the bi-weekly magazine – .

IAN: Hardly "bi."

VERA: I believe "semi" weekly is more correct.

CLIFF: Fine, "semi-weekly" magazine geared to the struggle for equal rights for those who are gay, "bi" sexual – not "semi" sexual – .

[Laughter]

CLIFF: – lesbian, trans-gendered and-or a transvestite. AKA: G-B-L-T-T.

NICK: Sounds like a sandwich.

ERIC: Oh, Jesus.

NICK: What? It's just a joke.

IAN: One I've made, myself. Though I did (snaps fingers). Makes for better emphasis.

CLIFF: Uh-huh. Welcome, Ian, snap or no snap.

[Audience applause]

CLIFF: Next is Rahim Condury, a former prosecutor for Melano County and now a criminal defense attorney. Talk about a switch hitter.

RAHIM: Do you refer to baseball or sexual preference?

NICK: Both, on this program.

[Light laughter & Applause]

CLIFF: Which brings us to Eric Larson, formerly an actor-slash-waiter and now – .

VERA: Have we seen you in something?

ERIC: I've been in a few movies. Nothing big. I...uh, I'm pretty much out of it, now.

IAN: So I read.

CLIFF: Eric joins us as someone who has intimate knowledge of the event we're about to discuss – the actions of the fans in Cincinnati against Bobby Carapisi, relief pitcher for The Golden State Griffins.

ERIC: I wouldn't call it intimate knowledge – .

CLIFF: Some knowledge, then.

ERIC: I just here to straighten out some misconceptions, help people to have a clearer idea of what probably happened with Bobby.

IAN: Because it happened to you?

ERIC: Yes. Basically.

CLIFF: Well, we're glad to have you here, Eric.

[Audience applause]

CLIFF: Let's look at the known story, so far. A few months ago, Bobby Carapisi went out to buy some ice cream, vanished for a few hours – .

ERIC: I think six hours is more than – .

CLIFF: Let me finish. A witness claimed to have seen him being attacked and called the police. Six hours later, he was found wandering down Santa Monica Boulevard, beaten and somewhat incoherent.

VERA: He wasn't merely incoherent; he was in shock.

RAHIM: It's my understanding he was severely beaten.

CLIFF: Yeah, well, I've heard it both ways.

NICK: Oh, c'mon, Cliff, I saw Bobby when he left the hospital, and even a week later he still looked pretty rough.

CLIFF: All I'm saying is – look, I don't want to pass judgment on this, yet, but – .

ERIC: But you don't believe his story.

CLIFF: That's not what I said.

ERIC: You may as well have.

CLIFF: Does anyone have any question with the facts I've laid out, so far?

ERIC: It's not what you're saying, it's how you're putting it.

CLIFF: Listen, before we jump into this discussion, let me finish. Bobby was beaten, no question. He spends five days in the hospital and

118

is on the disabled list for four weeks. He claims he doesn't remember anything that happened.

VERA: Which is not uncommon.

CLIFF: The hospital's being tight-lipped about Bobby's condition. The cops are being tight-lipped about the investigation. The Griffins are being tight-lipped about everything, even as rumors start flying. Bobby finally holds a press conference over a month after the initial assault, but the rumors don't stop so then he does a special interview on channel fourteen, his wife beside him, to specifically disclaim rumors that he was having a homosexual affair – .

NICK: He talked about a lot more than that.

CLIFF: Basically, but the one suggesting he jaunted over to West Hollywood to get some relief and got caught in a gay-bashing was the main – .

RAHIM: I think you're focusing too much on too small a part of his interview, Cliff.

IAN: I completely agree.

CLIFF: Okay, fine. But then comes this newspaper article wondering of Bobby was sexually assaulted and comparing Eric's accusations with what happened to – .

ERIC: The article came out before the interview.

CLIFF: By a few days. Big difference.

VERA: But an important one. He scheduled the interview as a direct response to the article.

ERIC: The show was broadcast a week later, not a few days.

CLIFF: Okay, okay, I did get that backwards.

ERIC: And the article mostly compared Bobby's treatment with mine. It didn't focus on the accusations, and actually suggested he was just attacked, not sexually assaulted.

IAN: But you're saying he was, aren't you?

ERIC: No, I'm not.

VERA: That article – many aspects were rather ill-informed.

RAHIM: I haven't read it. What was the essence of it?

CLIFF: Well, Mr. Larson, here, claimed that back in March he was abducted and sexually assaulted by three men, one of whom was William Barrow.

NICK: Hmph, Wheel Barrow.

IAN: Small wonder he chooses to go by his middle name.

VERA: How awful for you, Eric.

ERIC: Thanks.

CLIFF: In the article, Barrow claims that he purchased Eric's services – .

ERIC: Which is a lie.

CLIFF: – and was also gay-bashed while servicing Bobby Carapisi. Both times the sex was one-on-one and consensual.

ERIC: He says, which is a lie!

CLIFF: Maybe, but there's no evidence to the contrary. And then come the tabloids screaming about Bobby admitting to his wife he's gay.

VERA: Hardly a definitive source.

NICK: Maybe.

CLIFF: Bobby starts attacking his fans – .

NICK: You don't mean Dallas?

CLIFF: – and then comes Cincinnati.

NICK: Dallas was just one fan, Cliff, and he provoked it.

IAN: Whereas many of the fans in Cincinnati behaved like scum.

NICK: Now that – I don't completely agree with.

VERA: Oh, come now. Tossing "sex" toys onto the field? And bananas? And used prophylactics? Sending paper airplanes flying through the air made from pictures showing two men copulating? Calling out hideous phrases deriding the attack on Mr. Carapisi?

RAHIM: That's acceptable?

ERIC: Sports freaks think so.

NICK: Look, I'm not saying they didn't go a bit far – .

ERIC: A BIT far?!

NICK: – I'm just saying some of that behavior is normal for a ball game.

ERIC: Normal?!

CLIFF: No, I get Nick's meaning. The Cincinnati fans just wanted to win and – .

ERIC: So they brutalized the victim of a rape?

IAN: The "alleged" victim of a supposed – .

CLIFF: What they were playing was a psychological game against members of the opposing team. That's all. And there's nothing new about it.

NICK: Exactly. If Bobby'd been arrested for cocaine or accused of raping a woman, they'd have used that against him. Like with Keith Hernandez twenty-odd years ago, and Kobe Bryant.

VERA: Oh, no, no, no, that's not a valid comparison. Not when you factor in what Kobe's fans did to the woman who accused him.

IAN: And the homophobia involved in this. In Cincinnati. Why am I not surprised?

CLIFF: Look, I agree it got carried away, but verbal abuse is part of the game, isn't it?

NICK: Comes with the territory.

ERIC: No, no, no, no, no, you guys don't get it. This was more than just "verbal abuse."

VERA: Eric's right. If they had done to a woman what they did to Mr. Carapisi, in Cincinnati, they'd be drowning from the outrage rather than having people try to explain their actions away.

NICK: That's assuming he actually was the victim of a rape.

ERIC: He was.

IAN: So now you say it's true? I haven't seen any evidence of it.

ERIC: Are you with the DA's office? Have you been given access to the evidence they gathered?

IAN: What changed your mind? Because you said he wasn't.

ERIC: I didn't change my mind. I said, the article didn't say he was. I always thought he – I mean, I knew his story – I mean, I wanted to give him some space. To sort things out on his own.

IAN: Give space to a closet case who – .

ERIC: Bobby's straight!

IAN: – couldn't come out. We all know how homophobic the major sports teams are – football, basketball, baseball – you name it, they don't want no fags in it.

NICK: No argument there.

CLIFF: So you buy into the idea he was just out getting his rocks off, to put it crudely – .

ERIC: That's ridiculous.

CLIFF: – and got caught up in a gay-bashing?

IAN: And he's just trying to salvage his career. I doubt any of this would have happened had be been allowed to come out of the closet.

ERIC: Bobby is not gay.

IAN: You know that for a fact?

ERIC: Do you know for a fact that he is?

VERA: You know, he might not even consider himself gay. Many men do not consider fellatio the same as actual sex, therefore they can indulge in it without having to identify with – .

IAN: Honey, anything I do with a man is sex, trust me.

CLIFF: Okay, okay, on that note, we have to take a break. Be right back with more about Bobby Carapisi and Cincinnati.

[Break]

[Audience applause]

CLIFF: Okay, we're back with my guests, Ian Dekka, Dr. Vera Blumenthal, Rahim Condury, Eric Larson and Nicholas O'Crohan. Now let's give Eric's version of what happened a chance.

ERIC: Oh, thank you so much.

CLIFF: Now you said in the article these men forced you to ejaculate.

IAN: Oh, please, you can't force a man to do that.

VERA: Actually, it is possible, in some instances. Not all. To some men.

ERIC: And it's not like I enjoyed it.

IAN: I've enjoyed every one of my sexual encounters, ejaculations and all.

ERIC: It was not sex. It was a physical assault.

VERA: Eric is most definitely correct. Physical stimuli can bring about a physical response, despite the emotion of the moment being opposite to sexual interest. And that can include being brought to the point of ejaculation.

ERIC: Exactly. If you get hit in the stomach, wanting to throw up's got nothing to do with what you had for lunch.

NICK: Look, I can understand that in how it applies to a gay man, but – .

ERIC: Hey!

NICK: – to a heterosexual man? Who's being used in a way he thinks is sick? Is wrong for him? I don't know.

ERIC: Sexual orientation's got nothing to do with it.

VERA: It's a common misconception that a man's fear would override the sexual stimulation, but the fact is sometimes a highly-charged emotional experience actually increases the possibility of an erection.

CLIFF: And ejaculation?

VERA: As I said, sometimes. And with today's wide range of drugs which interrupt or enhance the male sexual experience – .

IAN: Eric, didn't you claim you were drugged?

ERIC: With Viagra and GHB.

VERA: The combination of which can remove conscious control of one's sexual – .

IAN: I thought Special K was involved in some way.

NICK: "Special K?"

RAHIM: Ketamine. An animal tranquilizer, which has a dissociative effect on the human body.

ERIC: They used that to gain control over me.

IAN: How? It takes it a few minutes for that to – .

ERIC: A combination of K and amyl nitrite.

IAN: Ni-TRATE.

VERA: Actually, ni-TRITE is correct. Amyl nitrate is a different substance from...oh, I forget the colloquial term? Pop-ups?

IAN: Poppers.

VERA: Yes! Poppers.

IAN: All of which is SO gay.

ERIC: Whatever! But it threw me off enough to where I couldn't coordinate a response to keep them from tying me up.

IAN: And then spend hours forcing you to enjoy yourself.

ERIC: I did not enjoy what happened – .

CLIFF: Is it possible for any man, anywhere to be coerced into gay sex?

ERIC: I keep telling you – it's not sex.

VERA: In response to your question, yes, it is possible.

NICK: I'm sorry, but I just don't buy it. Unless you have a history of – .

RAHIM: You don't believe a man can be sexually assaulted?

NICK: Not to where you enjoy it.

VERA: Rape is not enjoyable. For anyone.

CLIFF: But I've heard some women actually get off on being raped.

VERA: Which misrepresents the data we've gathered. There have been occurrences when a woman being sexually assaulted becomes aroused by – .

NICK: Oh, there's a straight boy fantasy.

VERA: – by the sexual contact. Nick. But it is not, I repeat, NOT, a pleasurable experience for her. In fact, it adds to her emotional turmoil. The exact same thing happens with males who are sexually assaulted. They begin to question their sexual identity.

RAHIM: Question their manhood.

VERA: Precisely. A man is raised to believe he should be able to fend off such an attack.

RAHIM: Which is not always possible. A case I'm handling, right now, deals with a young man who was sent to prison and was set upon by a half-dozen or more inmates. He wound up in the infirmary and has just tested HIV-Positive, when he was HIV-Negative prior to his incarceration.

NICK: But that's prison.

ERIC: So?

RAHIM: You don't mean to say you believe sexual assault should be accepted as an unwritten part of a convicted man's sentence, do you?

CLIFF: It's too much of a cliché to be anything else – .

RAHIM: Condemning to death a young man who was supposed to serve two years for a minor drug charge is hardly a cliché.

CLIFF: You know what I mean.

VERA: Cliff, please. It was a callous thing to say.

CLIFF: And true.

ERIC: And typical.

NICK: C'mon, they got drugs for AIDS now.

IAN: When you can afford them. And which work maybe fifty per-cent of the time and have severe side effects.

NICK: Okay, okay, but you have to agree – rape in prison is usually an assault on your butt, maybe even your mouth. But none of those guys give a (bleeped out) about getting you off. It's all about relieving their needs, not yours. Right?

VERA: Normally.

NICK: So it's different from this case. Which is where I'm coming from. You have to have a...a touchstone of some kind to let your body think what's being done to you can be fun.

CLIFF: I understand what you're getting at. I mean, Eric, you're gay, right? So you know what it's like to have sex with a man. You have a memory of it. Your body has a memory of it. Therefore, it's – .

ERIC: I don't get what you're getting at.

CLIFF: – almost understandable your body would react to the stimuli being used on you in a way that it has in the past, right?

VERA: That could be taken into account.

IAN: Just a few well-placed memories can make my body react.

CLIFF: Yet here we have this big, strong, heterosexual male who swears he's never had any other experiences with men.

IAN: I dunno. I hear he had a favorite uncle who was part of the clan, and whom he was really really fond of.

ERIC: Oh, you have got to be kidding me!

IAN: Happens all the time, honey.

CLIFF: Anyway, there are several reports that he admitted to his wife he ejaculated.

ERIC: That's not what he – .

VERA: He said he was forced to ejaculate.

NICK: Yeah!

ERIC: And it's coming from gossip rags. Who're out to make people think – .

IAN: So these men were doing things to him he'd never had done before, and he got off on it?

ERIC: He didn't get off on it.

NICK: Exactly. How?

ERIC: Have either of you ever been raped?

IAN: Does the legal definition of molestation count?

VERA: How old were you?

IAN: Thirteen.

RAHIM: It very much does count.

CLIFF: Was it similar to – .

IAN: Oh, here was no force involved. It was just my very married little league coach introducing me to the glories of...oh, oral copulation – can I say that on TV?

CLIFF: We're semi-cable – not "bi" cable – but don't go too colloquial on me.

[Audience laughter]

RAHIM: Semi-sensibilities must be protected.

IAN: I was just as much up for it as he was.

NICK: That is sick.

IAN: That's reality, honey. I've known I was gay since I was six. And this man was hot-hot-hot.

VERA: It's still rape, albeit statutory.

CLIFF: Thirteen-year-old boy with an adult male.

NICK: And he's bragging on it.

IAN: Damn straight. Pun intended.

ERIC: Then you're right, it's not the same – .

IAN: Are you telling me you didn't have sex till you – ?

ERIC: I knew when I was twelve, okay? But I – .

IAN: How nice. Finally we get the "I'm one of you" moment.

ERIC: No, I was never molested by an adult. I fooled around with boys my own age and – .

IAN: God, how tedious.

VERA: Ian, just because you found pleasure in the experience does not mean it was right to do.

IAN: Why not? Isn't rape really just a legal perception?

VERA: Oh, do not even go there – .

IAN: Why not?! I wanted him as much as he wanted me. The only reason it's rape is because the law says so.

RAHIM: With good cause. Look at the ongoing scandal in the Catholic Church, with pedophile priests using their position to seduce boys into committing acts they don't want to – .

IAN: Nobody made me do a damn thing I didn't want to.

RAHIM: – do and using the church's hierarchy to help them get away with it. Many of those boys are – .

VERA: And Girls.

RAHIM: – are seriously emotionally damaged by what happened to them.

ERIC: Anyone would be when they're forced to do something they don't want to do.

VERA: One in four girls and one in six boys, by some estimates.

CLIFF: And half the men in prison, if you believe what they say.

RAHIM: I don't appreciate you making rape in prison into a joke.

CLIFF: How can it be anything else? We'll be right back.

[Break]

[Audience Applause]

CLIFF: And we're back, and discussing rape in prison – .

VERA: Rape is too simple a term to use for what occurs in correctional facilities.

NICK: Yeah, a lot of sex behind bars qualifies more as trading favors than – .

IAN: Capitalism at work?

CLIFF: Well, the vast majority of cases reported as rape turn out to be more consensual than – .

RAHIM: Coercion still qualifies as rape.

CLIFF: I know, but – .

NICK: Coercion isn't the same as tying a guy down.

ERIC: It's emotional restraint.

CLIFF: Chains around my heart?

IAN: Oh, "Unchain my heart..."

ERIC: Why do you keep trivializing this and – ?!

CLIFF: Eric, Eric, uh, now, as I understand, you believe Bobby was...uh, well, treated in the same manner as you.

ERIC: Yeah. Yeah, that's what it seems like.

CLIFF: Have you spoken with him?

ERIC: No.

IAN: You're kidding?

ERIC: No. He was out of town when I learned he was – .

NICK: He didn't leave town till after he learned the article was about to be published.

ERIC: I didn't know he was the other guy. Not till Pete came back to me – .

CLIFF: That's Peter Zamora, the reporter who wrote the article.

ERIC: Yeah. He'd tried to get the Griffins to give him some info but they stonewalled him. Then Bobby split and Pete came back to me. To get more detailed information. He found out from the police reports Allen had been interviewed by the police in connection with Bobby's –.

CLIFF: He also spoke with Barrow first, right?

ERIC: Yeah. And Allen gave him this (bleeped out) about it being consensual between him and me, and then that it was just him and Bobby. But the fact that here's two different men saying the same thing about him...about Allen...made Pete wonder – .

RAHIM: How many men attacked you?

ERIC: Three.

CLIFF: Only says one in the police report.

ERIC: No, it doesn't.

CLIFF: I read the report, Eric. There's only one name.

ERIC: Read it, again. You'll see I told them, three.

NICK: So you're saying, it was also three men who attacked Bobby?

ERIC: Yeah. And Bobby says it, too.

IAN: Your stories match just a bit too closely.

ERIC: So?

IAN: So it sounds more like a coordinated effort to hide something than – .

ERIC: I've never met Bobby Carapisi. Never even talked to him.

IAN: Sure, honey. Whatever you say.

ERIC: So what is it you're suggesting?

IAN: Nothing. Nothing. I just think...well, it's weird that three men would get together not just to kidnap someone but to tie him down and take turns with him, when you can find someone so easily who'd be into that and would get you just as satisfied.

RAHIM: Rape is not about satisfaction. It's about power.

VERA: And multiple attackers are more common when males are assaulted.

NICK: In prison.

RAHIM: It happens in the community, as well. Much as the police like to pretend it does not.

CLIFF: But the DA's office also lists just one attacker.

ERIC: There were three, Cliff. Why do you keep coming back to that?

CLIFF: Just trying to get a straight answer from you.

IAN: Pun intended?

[Laughter]

ERIC: Allen was the only one I could identify.

CLIFF: And they declined to prosecute him. The DA's office did.

ERIC: Yeah. But they also decline to prosecute about half the cases – .

VERA: Wasn't evidence of the assault gathered?

ERIC: Yeah.

RAHIM: Yet, it still became his word against yours?

ERIC: Yes.

VERA: Also, in the interview, Bobby claims he remembers nothing about the attack, and insists he was not sexually assaulted.

NICK: Yeah. Even he suggested you're just out for money, Eric.

ERIC: I was attacked in March. You think I was just waiting around till somebody else got hit by Allen and his – ?

IAN: Y'know, this sounds an awful lot like what happened in San Francisco a few years ago.

CLIFF: What's that?

IAN: The winner of a gay leather contest at some bar was picked up by a fan after the contest was over. They went home, got things going then he yelled rape because things went a bit too far. Police refused to prosecute – .

RAHIM: Police gather evidence; the district attorney's office decides whether or not to prosecute.

IAN: Whatever, but it became one man's word against another, too.

ERIC: If a woman says "no" at any time and a man keeps going, it's considered rape. Why not with a man?

IAN: It's legal definitions, again.

VERA: If anyone involved in a sexual situation wants to stop, then you stop. Anything beyond that is forcible – .

IAN: Oh, please! This is sex, not geometry. It's a very intense emotional experience, where things can get carried away. I mean, we're not robots; we're human beings. How many times have any of us gone home with someone who looked like a movie star at two in the morning, but with dawn's clear light turned into a toad and made us want to kick ourselves?

ERIC: That's not what happened.

IAN: Says you. But you have nothing to back your story up.

RAHIM: Except it happened to another man.

CLIFF: Eric says. The so-called victim doesn't.

NICK: Right, 'cause Bobby ain't talking, no more. To anybody.

CLIFF: And that's the big problem here. With the whole situation. Nobody knows what really happened.

RAHIM: But too many people have made up their minds that they do know.

ERIC: And you wonder why Bobby's not talking.

CLIFF: He just vanished into his gated community with his wife – .

VERA: Perfectly understandable, considering the trauma he's suffered and the uproar that's followed.

ERIC: Jesus, what they did to him. What they're still doing.

CLIFF: So you come down on the side of the fans being in the wrong?

NICK: I'm telling you, there's nothing all that unusual about their actions, and it's something he should have handled.

RAHIM: But even you noted they went too far.

NICK: Throwing crap on the field, yes. But enough to warrant a two game forfeit?

CLIFF: I hear Scott, the catcher for Cincinnati, he's asked to be traded.

NICK: Stupid move on his part.

VERA: I think he's being very principled in the – .

NICK: No one'll pick up his contract. Not if he dumps on a great team like Cincie over something as dumb as this.

ERIC: Dumb?!

NICK: Yeah, dumb. Whatever happened that night with Bobby, if he wasn't ready to handle the crowd he shouldn't have gone out on the field. He should've known the story'd be used against him. It's part of the deal in sports, these days.

VERA: I hardly find that admirable.

NICK: I'm not saying it is. I'm saying it's reality. And Scott's going to get hit by it, too.

ERIC: Because he said what happened wasn't right?

NICK: Two of my colleagues have already wondered if Scott's got another reason for speaking out, if you know what I mean.

IAN: Honey, I was putting two and two together the moment his mouth popped open.

ERIC: Oh. Oh, that is just plain evil.

CLIFF: Now I don't think, uh – .

NICK: I'm not saying I agree with it, but reality is, some people're going to wonder.

RAHIM: Wonder what?

IAN: "Scott and Bobby, sitting in a tree, K-I-S-S-I-N-G." And look which one pitches and which one catches. The punch lines are just too adorable.

VERA: Can't we even consider the possibility Bobby's telling the truth? That he was merely beaten and not sexually assaulted? Is it that hard for us to let go of the idea?

IAN: Or admit that maybe there's more truth to the rumors than some of us're willing to admit. Eric.

CLIFF: But Scott's got a wife and three kids.

IAN: So? It only goes to show just how deep the closet is in major league sports.

ERIC: What the (bleeped out) is going on here? Is the only way you people can face the idea that a man can get raped is if he's queer or in jail!? Mother (bleeped out). I wish I'd never said a (bleeped out) thing.

IAN: But you did, didn't you?

ERIC: You shut the (bleeped out) up, you (bleeped out) bitch.

CLIFF: Whoa!

IAN: I'm not the whore at this round table, honey.

ERIC: Hey, hey, hey!

CLIFF: Guys, guys.

IAN: I'm not the slut out to grab some publicity for herself – .

ERIC: Publicity?!

CLIFF: Guys, c'mon, let's not – .

IAN: – maybe get a book deal or movie-of-the-week out of it –

ERIC: You think I like talking about this?!

IAN: – And screw what it does to the gay community.

CLIFF: Hey, sit down! Both of – .

IAN: Or maybe you're just after another payoff, but this time from Bobby-baby. To keep quiet about your times together.

ERIC: You are a (bleeped out) whack-job! Seeing queer where there ain't no queer. Bobby's straight and decent and – .

IAN: Oh, don't go all Virgin Mary on us, honey; doesn't match your chosen profession.

I threw my water at him. Plastic bottle and all. Didn't hit him but got him wet enough to howl like a pissed off tom-cat. The only reason we didn't go head to fist was Cliff grabbed me and Nick grabbed Ian. And then shoved us into different areas of the studio. Of course, the audience thought it was all part of the act, like "Jerry Springer" or something, so they howled and applauded...and probably would have, even if one of us had knifed the other and spilled guts everywhere.

They edited it out of the broadcast and cut to a still ruffled Cliff thanking everyone involved and then summarizing our commentary into a simple "yes" versus "no" situation – Dr. Blumenthal, Rahim Condury, Ian Dekka and I said Cincinnati deserved any punishment given them; Nicholas O'Crohan and Cliff Morrison felt the punishment outweighed the crime. And tomorrow's guests would discuss the current state of affairs in Washington DC as regards passage of yet another anti-gay bill offered up by the GOP, with the Democrats flowing right along with them, and how it might be affected by the uproar over Bobby C. Included would be a Republican who'd denounced Bobby Carapisi on the floor of the House at the exact same time we were taping.

That show taped but didn't air, of course. How could it, after what happened, next?

The umps were so pissed about what the crowd pulled on me, they forfeited the game to The Griffins. That didn't sit so well with the Cincie fans, so a mini-riot broke out. But all that did was get the commissioner to forfeit the next two games Cincie played, too.

Chief sent me home, that night. Alone. Had armed guards take me to a private field an' hired a little jet to fly me straight into Van Nuys 'stead of Ontario. That gave me five nice long hours to remember everything. Rehash it in my brain. Remember every fuckin' detail till I made full use of the plane's bar. But even that didn't help; it just made the time pass. I didn't even start to get a buzz off it.

I called Aunt T an' she come get me. When she pulled up, I got in the car an' she put her hand on my arm to let me know she knew. I was grateful; that way I didn't have to talk all the way home.

There were some news crews camped at the community's entrance, but we zipped right past 'em. I guess they got some video of me, but I didn't care. Didn't even think about it.

Aunt T lead me in the house an' told Donna to call her if we needed anything. Donna just nodded. She never looked at me. She kept all her attention on Aunt T, an' when she was gone, Donna just went upstairs. I didn't. I just walked out on the deck an' sat down on a lounger an' stayed there, all night.

Y'know, the only time I was really glad we lived in a gated community was when I got back from that...that hellhole. The front guards kept most the news bastards outside the community an' away from my house. A few still snuck over the fence, but they got caught real easy. That's when the committee brought in extra guards with dogs an' posted signs warnin' 'em that they'd get arrested if they was caught. I don't think the signs mattered so much, but the dogs sure did.

So did my neighbors yellin' at 'em to get lost. Steve an' Adrianna Moskowitz, this really great couple what live two doors down from us, would come over to fill us in on the – how'd he put it? – uh, the "ebb an' flow of the sewerage crowd." Yeah. They're the ones who told me 'bout how this guy who called himself a "man of God" started picketin' 'cross the street from the gate. Said he was from Kansas or somethin' an' he brought some more people with him an' they were holdin' up signs that said some really dumb shit, though they wouldn't tell me exactly what. An' since I wasn't watchin' the news, I never found out. He split after a few days 'cause one of his people tossed a cig into the brush an' started a fire. Almost took out a house. This one fire captain told 'em they either go or go to jail for arson...so they left. I never saw 'em.

An' then there's my next door neighbors on both sides, who kept watch for sneakers. Charlie Sandoval, on my left, he caught this one guy climbin' a tree behind my house, an' held a gun on him till the cops arrived. His wife, Karen, taped it all on her cell; so when the guy started claimin' that Charlie said he'd shoot him, she turned it over an' showed the guy was a liar. I watched the whole thing. It was sweet. An' on my right was Stasi, used to be big in tennis. He started acceptin' all our mail an' deliveries an' goin' through 'em to weed out the really nasty shit after Donna opened up one with a picture two guys makin' it, with my head pasted over the guy who was gettin'...the guy who...who was catchin', not pitchin'. Stasi turned the death threats an' other crap over to the cops, an' blasted the news scum at the gate, on camera, more than a couple times. Problem is, it made us prisoners in that place.

Not that I cared. I needed the quiet. I needed bein' left alone. Needed to stay away from the paper an' the T-V an' the radio an' everything there was that could remind me of what happened in Cincie. I'd sit on the deck an' nurse a beer an' gaze 'cross the hills an' let the sun bake me an' I got to where I didn't think. The day'd just pass...an' then I'd watch this fantastic sunset. I'd always loved sunsets. It's like they're sayin', it's time to rest after a long hard day. An' I stay there into the night. Sometimes, when I didn't crash on the couch, I'd sleep there. God, it felt so good...so peaceful...so easy I could of stayed there the rest my life.

An' Donna – she...she left me alone. Didn't talk to me for a whole day, once. Not like she didn't know what to say, but like she didn't want to say what she was thinkin'. I could tell. I know her. She'd be workin' in the house or takin' care of Priss or waterin' the plants an' wind up walkin' towards me an' then realize I'm home an' stop walkin' an' turn around to do somethin' else. All without thinkin'. She never did that before. An' she made sure Priss left me alone. Once upon a time, all of it would of bothered me...but it didn't, now. 'Cause I knew what she was thinkin'.

I knew.

Ma flew out to be with us after a couple days. Help Donna out. Be there for the baby, even though he wasn't due till next month. An' she told Mary Frances she'd just have to cope with Pop, no ifs, ands or buts. Aunt T picked her up at the airport. If me or Donna'd gone, it would have been nuts. As it was, Aunt T had to almost ram her way through the crowd to get past the gate. Photographers were crushin' against the car an' slappin' the hood an' screamin' all kinds of shit tryin' to get a picture or video of big bad Bobby's momma for the shit-rags or that night's news. Show the world the woman who gave birth to the evil little bastard what shit on the perfect sport of baseball – not my phrase; Langston's...from before...

Uh, when they finally got to the house, Aunt T was rantin', "Mother-fuckin' sons-of-bitches, bastards, every one! Goddamn animals! No, no, that's a curse against animals, to compare 'em to those...those... those snakes. Those worms! Bastards. All of 'em!"

For the first time in my life, Ma agreed with every word she said. Never once got that disappointed look on her face at Aunt T's bad language. Even when Aunt T went off crazier after findin' they'd put a dent in Raymon's Chrysler. It was priceless.

Ma settled in real quick. Made Donna stop fidgetin' an' rest more. Took care of Priss. Made sure I was sloppin' on suntan lotion twice a day. An' hugged me, lots. Touched my hair. Much as she could. Whenever she could. I let her...but I didn't hug back, an' I think that hurt her.

I dunno what I was doin', just sittin' there. No...I do know. I ain't that dumb. You get run off the field in the middle of a game. You get told a commercial you were gonna shoot is "postponed indefinitely." You get un-invited to tapin's of shows for charity. You got guys on your team won't even look at you, let alone talk to you. You gotta figure your career's over. Done. No more.

That meant the end of this lifestyle. Oh, I made some coin, but lots of it went in our house an' that was down in the market. Cars. Investments. Savin's for college for Priss. Trips to see Pop an' Ma much as we could. No way I can keep that up on a regular salary. The house'd have to go, if we could sell it. But Donna was good with money so that wouldn't be all that bad.

So then what? Where could I go to make a livin' for me an' my wife an' kids? Where could I go that I wouldn't be hounded or whispered about or made fun of? I'd have to change my name. Keep a low profile. Live completely different. Wouldn't be so hard. If I let the weight keep packin' on, six months from now you wouldn't even know me.

So I guess that's what I was doin' there: tryin' to accept that my life wasn't mine, no more. It was somethin' I had to hide away an' lie about till I was dead. Not exactly what I planned. I kept tellin' myself that at least I got four good years in doin' what I loved. Almost five. Most people don't even get four days. But it still cut deep...an' I hated that it was happenin'.

After almost a week, ma come out an' sat beside me. I heard her, but I didn't look at her. Then I noticed how quiet the house was. Donna must of taken Priss down the playground down the hill. I hoped they'd have fun.

It took Ma a while to work up to sayin' somethin'. I hear her huff an' sigh prob'ly a dozen times before she said, "Bobby, I talked to Donna."

An' I'm thinkin', Oh, shit, here it comes.

She goes on with, "She had some stupid...stupid ideas. Ideas a girl as smart as her shouldn't have. I pointed out a few things to her and...and she's sorry. She's sorry, Bobby. She knows she was wrong to...to wonder. To doubt you. And now she's afraid to talk to you. She's afraid if she says anything to you, you'll fall apart, again."

She tell you I hit her, Ma? She tell you I'm that kind of asshole?

She kept on. "She's scared, Bobby. She's scared, not just for herself and her children, but for you. She needs to see that you're strong, again. And you are strong, baby."

Ah, Ma...always so nice...so supportin'. But this time you're way off base.

She got closer to me; I could hear the chair move, an' she said, "You're a good, decent, loving man who's stronger than this. I know you are. I've seen it in you all your life. So you have to stop this. You have to stop these silences. You have to talk to you wife. Show her you're strong, again."

Talk to my wife? What about? How I let our life get ruined? How I got our future smashed to bits? You think I'm strong? So did I, once upon a time. But if I was then how could I of let this happen? Talk to her, Ma? No need. She knows everything she needs to know 'bout me – an' it ain't pretty.

I heard Ma sigh. Guess my not lookin' at her gave her my answer. So she kept on with, "Bobby, you have to stop this. It's not doing you any good. Not doing anybody any good."

I still didn't answer her. Still didn't look at her. Just kept starin' out over the hills. Fact is, I wasn't even really thinkin' 'bout what she was sayin', anymore. The words were there, but they didn't mean nothin' to me. It's just ma sittin' beside me, chattin'.

She kept on. "Bobby, listen to me. I'm your mother. An' I'm tellin' you – you gotta get hold of yourself. You got responsibilities. A wife. Two kids. You gotta think about more than just you, right now. You gotta think about them. Be strong for them, if not for yourself."

Yeah, sure, ma. Been there. Done that. Found out it's just that easy. Yeah, you just flick off the switch an' all your troubles go bye-bye. No biggie. An' now if you don't mind, I'll just have another sip of my brewski.

She moved in closer. Touched my arm.

"Baby, please. At least try. Just a little. Just a little, today. Just for an hour. Get up. Get a bath. Walk down the hill an' play with your daughter. That's all. You're her father. She misses you. Don't you want to be with her?"

'Course I do, ma. Love her more than my life. Let those devils do what they did so I could see her again. Her an' Donna. Look what it got me. 'Nother sip, please.

Ma moved her chair 'round in front of me. Blocked my view. Made me look at her. Holy Mary, the look on her face. So full of hurt an'...an' fear...an' worry. It almost ripped my heart in two. Almost.

"Tell me what he did to you."

That jolted me, a little.

"I already know. Donna told me."

She fuckin' WHAT?!

"I want to hear it from you. You tried to tell me, once. I know. I see it, now. That day you came in an' I was cooking dinner for Rich. I should of known something was wrong. Give me a second chance, baby. Tell me now."

Tell my mother? That? It's bad enough she thinks she knows what happened, but she wants me to spell it out for her?! Myself? No fuckin' way! Shit!

"Robert Anthony, don't you look at me like that! I will accept anything you tell me. You know I will."

"No." The word popped out 'fore I knew I was sayin' it.

"I don't care what it is. I don't care how you put it. Just say it! You tell me what those sons-of-bitches did to you. You tell me."

I moved back, I was so shocked at what ma said. She called them sons-of-bitches! My mother! Shit! That almost jolted me into next Sunday.

"Please. Baby, you got it all bottled up, inside, an' it's killin' you. I can see it. You gotta let it out, Bobby."

"Can't." Again, the word came from nowhere. "Look what happened with Donna...an'...an'..."

Ma took my face in her hands. Tears were in her eyes.

"Bobby, Donna is a wonderful girl...in most ways. But you remember how she was when she learned I let your Uncle Tommy watch you kids? After my great big stupid brother, Paulie, filled her in on him? It's like...like she thought I was out of my mind. Like I was handing my sons over to a child molester. She couldn't understand that I knew Tommy loved you boys so much, he'd commit murder before he'd let anything happen to you."

Yeah, I remember. Good ol' Uncle Tommy. An' ma was right: Donna did get all crazy-weird about him. Never wanted to be around him. Didn't understand how rock solid he was.

Aw, shit, ma...why'd you bring him up? Bring all that shit back to me? I didn't need it, not now.

Aw, shit!

I got up an' walked away from her.

"Bobby..."

Her voice ripped into me, so I had to tell her, "Gonna take a shower, ma."

An' that's what I did. Ran it hot as I could stand it. Stripped off an' scrubbed. Once. Twice. Again. Not thinkin' 'bout it. Not deliberate. It's like, I...I didn't remember for sure if I got everywhere, so I'd start over. I was in there half an hour, I guess, before I got back to a blank mind. Then I dried off an' dressed.

Well...tried to dress. Nothin' I had fit, no more. Not around the waist. Even my Jockeys felt tight. So I pulled on a pair of sweats that weren't too small for me an' some sandals an' headed out the house.

I wandered down the hill towards the park. A big open place where all the kids get to play an' run around like dogs. It's nice there. Feels safe for 'em. The road curves a bit an' there's trees along it an' I used to love joggin' down the hill an' back up, even in the middle of summer. I was halfway there when I heard somebody runnin' down the hill, behind me, yellin' "Bobby! Bobby!" I tensed an' looked back to find Charlie comin' at full throttle, his cell phone in his hand.

"Bobby! Karen just called me! She tried to get you but your mom said you'd left! It's Donna! Down at the park! She's called an ambulance an'..."

I was runnin' at top speed 'fore he finished. I whipped 'round the curve an' found the playground in the middle of the green space an' saw a tiny group of women huddled 'round someone lyin' on the ground an' I started sceamin', "Donna! Donna!"

Suddenly I saw her holdin' onto Karen. Her clothes were bloody an' she was bawlin' an' then I didn't see nothin' else but her. I slid up beside her an' tried to figure out where to hold her but Holy Mary there was so much blood, I was afraid I'd hurt her if I touched her.

She saw me an' whipped her arms around my neck, cryin', tryin' to talk but not makin' any sense. I just held an' started whisperin', "It's okay, baby. It's okay. It's gonna be okay. It's gonna be fine."

I looked at Karen. "Where's the fuckin' ambulance?!"

"I'm still with 9-1-1," she said back. "It's stopped at the gate. The reporters crowded around it and some of them tried to ride it down and the guards said it's like a riot, up there. They called the police for help."

The woman who was holdin' Priss said, "The scum."

Some other woman chimed in, "Where's police brutality when you need it?"

Then we heard the tiny wailin' of the ambulance an' it sounded like a cop car was with it. Sure enough, two years later, a black an' white escorted the red truck up the park an' the paramedics ran out an' took over. Donna's still cryin' an' screamin', so they started shootin' questions at me.

"What's her name?"

"Donna. Donna Carapisi."

"How far along is she?"

"Eight months."

Donna started screamin', "I'm gonna lose it! I'm gonna lose it!"

An' I'm all, "No, no, Donna, he's just comin' early, that's all." Like I knew shit.

His woman partner started tryin' to get Donna to lay back, sayin', "Donna. Donna, I need you let go of your husband. C'mon, honey, let's lie down. Donna, c'mon. Let's calm down. Let's relax. Honey, listen to me. We're going to do everything we can to take care of you and your baby, okay? But you have to calm down, honey. You have to focus. Deep breaths. C'mon. Deep breaths. Slowly. Slowly. Now let go of... of...?"

She looked at me an' I popped out with, "Bobby," an' I could of kissed her for not knowin' who I was. Or not carin'.

"Let go of Bobby an' let's lie back, okay?"

Donna was still cryin', but she wasn't hysterical, no more. She nodded an' started workin' at regainin' control, so I shifted around to let her head rest on my knees. Then both paramedics got busy with her. The guy had a hospital on the phone an' he was readin' out all kinds of stuff as they worked Donna over. I didn't understand a word of it, but I knew it was dead serious. Then he looked over at a stretch of open park an' I heard him say into his phone, "Yeah, I see an area that's big enough. Looks like a baseball diamond."

I looked 'round...an' saw there was a softball field behind me. Never noticed it, before.

Then the guy paramedic tugged my arm an' he told me, "We're calling in a helicopter to ferry you to the E-R. That crowd by the gate's too unpredictable."

An' Donna's all, "Bobby...Bobby..."

I jolted to look back at her. She was soundin' real scared, so I leaned in an' whispered in her ear, "It's gonna be okay, baby. They're sendin' a chopper. It's the fastest way to the hospital. I'll be with you the whole time. Okay?"

"You...you sure?"

I nodded like some dumb schmuck actin' like he knows what the hell he's doin'.

Then she's wonderin', "Where's Priss?"

I looked up an' saw ma takin' her from that lady an' said, "Ma's got her. She's takin' her up the house. Nice an' safe, okay? Got nothin' to worry about, there. Just worry 'bout you."

Then I saw ma castin' me an' Donna a look so scared an' painful, I sank inside. She knew what was happenin'. She'd been through it once...no, twice. Between Rich an' me, an' after Mary Frances, when the doctors told her not to have no more kids. Last come near killin' her. So fuckin' near. But right then, I wouldn't believe it. I mean, I didn't really...I mean...shit, I knew it in my head, but not in my heart. I couldn't believe it in my heart. God couldn't do that to me, too. Not that.

But when the woman paramedic said, "We're equidistant between Cedars an' St. Mark's," I didn't let her say anything more.

"St. Mark's," I said. "We're goin' to St. Mark's." Catholic Hospital. Priest on call along with the doctors. Somebody to...to give comfort an' to...to baptize an'...an' just in case...just in case...to give last rites.

Everybody was real gentle when they told me 'bout Donna. Like they felt it would make things easier. "She's restin' quietly." "All's fine. We gave her a sedative." "She'll be sleepin' for a while." "Why don't you go get some rest?" Yap, yap, yap. I don't remember sayin' anything in answer, not once. I think all I did was shake my head or nod it or give a gentle smile back at them.

But it didn't change the fact that my son was gone. "Spontaneous miscarriage." "Still birth." "No real damage." "Can try again, after a while." All nice an' sweet an' oh so carin', all of it. But still with one cold cruel message – my son was gone. Dead 'fore he was born.

He was never gonna play catch, like Pop did with me, a couple times an' like I'd swore I'd do with him every chance I got. Never gonna be taught how to shave, like Uncle Tommy taught me. I was never gonna hold his hand as we crossed the street. Never ride him on my shoulders. Never watch him grow up. He was gone. No, not gone; he just never made it to this station. An' I can't even begin to tell you how cold an' alone an' empty that made me feel. An' guilty. 'Cause it was my fault. I knew it. Know it. I could see it in their eyes. Hear it in their voices. Even Father Dominguez. He's the priest at St. Mark's. He said all the right things. All the crap he has to hand out, but I could tell. I could hear it echo in his words. "How could you let this happen? How?"

All the gentle people finally left me 'lone with Donna, in her room. She was sleepin', lookin' small an' delicate an' so much like Priss it ripped my heart. I know I should o' been in chapel prayin' for my little boy. Should o' been beggin' God to take him back. Beggin' God for forgiveness. But all I could do is watch Donna breathe. So soft.

Soft.

Soft.

So I just sat there, waitin' for her to wake up. Waitin' for her to come back to me. I think I knew even then that – that even if she did come back...it'd only be to say good-bye. But I still sat there. An' I waited.

An' I waited.

An' I waited.

I cannot say if I had any kind of thoughts the entire time. Not even a memory. It's like I was this computer that'd crashed from overload an' this one image was on the screen an' the cursor was blinkin' but you couldn't move it...you couldn't click it...you couldn't get it to do a damn thing. It just waited for you to shut it down so it could begin, again. That was me. That was my whole life, right then.

What could I have done to make things better? Different? I fuckin' go out for ice cream an'...an'...shit. I should of gone to the valley. Should of turned left instead of right. Should of told myself it don't matter what kind of lime sherbet it is so long as it's lime sherbet. Instead...now...I dunno what to say. Dunno what to think. Dunno what to do except wonder what could I have done to make things better? No answers come. I don't think any ever will, now.

Finally, Donna stirred...an' slowly come 'round. Even wakin' up after somethin' as rotten as this, she looked sweet an' innocent an' gentle, like Priss. Her eyes just sort of half opened. She took in the room, first. Then she looked out the window at the view. Then she looked at me. An' looked away. No change of expression to give me any idea what she was thinkin'. No sigh or sound of any kind to let me know what to expect. She just looked away.

But I knew. I knew.

We stayed like that for...I dunno, a few minutes, a few hours... then she said in this voice so soft it cut deeper than a knife, "Why didn't he kill you? I could've lived with that. It would've been hard, but I'd have made do. People would have been kind instead of vicious. I'd have had sympathy instead of questions. And no matter what they'd discovered about what he did to you...or with you...or made you do...or you enjoyed doing...I'd have had kindness instead of cruelty. And our son would have been willing to be born. He should have killed you."

Still just "he." Still just the one guy.

Then she looked at me an' said, "That's why he left, you know. That's why I miscarried so late in the term. My son would rather die than live his life with a fag for a father." She looked away from me, again, an' said, "Why didn't you make him kill you? Our boy could have lived with that. So could I."

I still don't feel anything 'bout what she said. Not one single solitary emotion...unless bein' numb is one. I just listened to her. Let her talk. Let her drift back to sleep. Then I got up an' went to her bed an' leaned over an' kissed her on the cheek. Just barely. Then I walked out the room.

Aunt T was in the hallway, an' I could see how she'd heard some of what Donna said. Man, she looked a wreck. She put a hand to my face an' said, "Bobby, don't hold this against her. She's hurt and confused and doesn't know what she's saying. She probably won't even remember saying it."

I smiled an' said, "Sure, Aunt T. I know." I held her face in my hands an' kissed her forehead an' said, "I'm gonna go, now."

"Yeah, baby," she said.

"Can I use your car?"

"Sure, baby. Go to my place. Get some rest. It'll help you. Help you both. You'll see. It's Raymon's Three Hundred on One-A, right by the elevator. I'll call you when Donna wakes up, again."

She give me her keys. I just smiled an' walked away. Then I went down the hospital store an' bought this tape recorder an' some tapes. An' I been drivin' all over town tellin' my story into 'em. Dunno why I'm tellin' it. It's not like it's gonna change anything. Not like anybody cares. Not really. They just like me hurtin'. They like that I'm damaged, now. Dunno what I did to deserve it...but that's the truth of it.

The whole fuckin' truth of it.

So now I'm sittin' on top this parking garage in Santa Monica, watchin' the sun set over the ocean. An' it's pretty. All blue an' purple an' yellow an' orange an' gold. An' the clouds catch every bit of the color. The water's gentle. It's rollin' up to the beach way below like it's waitin' for me to say somethin'. Maybe come join it. An' there's seagulls an' pigeons still driftin' in the sky. Sparrows. Finches.

I love sunsets. They're so peaceful, even the big splashy ones. Takes me back to the first day I met Donna. An' we went down-a-shore. Like it's the first day of my life, then. Guess I was hopin' it'd...it might bring me some...peace. Or...or some kind of...of...understandin'. Or.

Or.

Oh, Jesus, Ma, I'm so sorry! I should of been born with your strength, should of...should of got Aunt Teresa's fight, should of never had any dreams, what a stupid fuck I was, dreamin', please, God, please don't hold this against me, you can't hold it against me, please, I know it's a sin but everything in me is shredded to bits an' I got nothin' left, nothin', nothin' but this echo where my life used to be an' I'm not strong enough to build it up, again, I swear to you, I tried.

I tried.

I tried.

I tried so hard an' I almost did it. I almost did even though he... they...aw, holy Mary, even now I can't say it, can't face it, that one little stinkin' word. It. It's not what guys do to each other. It's never what a guy ought to make another guy do but he...they did it to me, they tore away everything an' made me nothin' an' I'm so lost an' so confused an' so ripped up an' everybody's so quiet, I don't know what to say, anymore. What I can say. The only words I know that mean anything is...is those six awful terrible brutal words – Bobby, Bobby, Bobby's ass is easy. That's all that echoes in my mind, anymore, all that echoes in my soul, no more joy, no more future, just those six words an' I try to think, but they're all that fills my mind an' I try to speak, but they're all that wants to be said an' I don't know how to stop it an' I don't know what else to do so please, God, please don't hold this against me, please, please, please.

Please.

Please.

Oh, Jesus, oh...Holy Mary, mother of God, the Lord is with thee...with...with...I...I...oh...

Oh.

Oh, wow.

There's a...a line cuttin' through the sky. A...a jet contrail, that's it. Two of 'em. Startin' all of a sudden in...in this...this pink an' gold an' white, first one, then the other, angled to each other, like an X.

Wow.

First time I ever saw one like that. First time I ever saw one, I was four. I thought somebody was cuttin' a hole in the sky. Pop tried for hours to calm me down...till Uncle Tommy told me it was just God markin' a spot for...for the next shootin' star.

Oh.

Oh, God. Is that what you're doin'? You markin' a spot in the sky for me? You...you openin' a way up for me? Is that what you're doin'? Sayin' it's okay?

Is that it?

Thank you.

Thank you.

Oh, man.

I ain't used up all of "side A" on this last tape. I better rewind it so nobody thinks there's nothing on the flip side.

"BENEDICTION"

I was on Pico waiting to turn down Barrington when I heard. It was the middle of morning rush hour and I'd just spent ten minutes trying to get through the intersection. During it all, some character on NPR had expounded unmercifully on how the Three Rivers Gorges Dam in China was responsible for a typhoon that wiped out close to ten percent of Bangladesh, again. Then came their trumpet-like music... followed by this announcer's voice, soft and purring with importance.

"You may recall we devoted part of yesterday's program to the situation concerning Bobby Carapisi and his deplorable treatment at the hands of rabid baseball fans in Cincinnati, recently. It had been revealed that he was sexually assaulted after being kidnapped and was viciously beaten, but the tabloids had turned it into a case of a closeted man being nothing more than mugged. Instead of being greeted with kindness and understanding, he was driven from the playing field by non-stop cat-calls suggesting he had wanted to be raped, as well as various objects and pictures being tossed at him. Well...we have just learned that Robert Anthony Carapisi, relief pitcher for the Golden State Griffins, leapt to his death from the top of a Santa Monica parking structure, yesterday evening. When asked if Mr. Carapisi's suicide was connected to what happened in Cincinnati, police spokesman Carlos

Delgado replied, 'Isn't it obvious?' Bobby Carapisi leaves behind a wife and daughter. He was twenty-six years old."

Every word blew into my soul with flaming crystals of ice. I think I forgot to breathe, for a while, because the world grew bright and blistering and merged into this cold white nothingness. And I began to sob. Not weep. Not cry. Not bawl. I was as quiet as death as I shook and gasped and pounded the steering wheel and dashboard and door and anything else my fists could reach as tears drifted down my cheeks.

He was dead. He was dead. He was dead. Three words screaming 'cross my brain, over and over and over...and with them the knowledge that I was responsible for it. I killed him. I lead him up to the top of that garage and I pushed him over and I watched him fall and fall and fall, twisting and trying to grasp at anything to keep from hitting the ground and I saw it again and again and again. It was hell. I had died and been sent to hell for my sin, the worst sin a man can do to another, the sin of destroying his hope to the point of crushing the life from him. I was evil. I was filth. I was the devil's own disciple and I screamed and railed and wept over it until the whiteness returned to blank out the images of suffering and death.

Car horns blared. People shrieked curses that I wasn't doing the decent thing and taking the turn like a real Angeleno. Not one of them gave a fuck that I was dying – that I was lost in the total and complete whiteness of death, with no ground beneath me or ceiling above me or anyone to hold me and soothe me and guide me back to myself...guide me out of the terror enveloping my very soul as I twisted and turned and begged for someone...anyone to help me...please, God, help me!

I don't know how long I was there – out of control in grief for a man I did not know, could never know – when a tapping sound drifted past me. A man – I think it was a man – was at my door's window, knocking on the glass with his ring. He must have thought I was freaked out on a downer mixed with vodka and upset over a bug I'd just crushed against my radiator, but he knew I wasn't going anywhere in that condition. So he got my door open, guided me out of the car and over to a curb.

I was still lost. Still struggling to escape the white white darkness. But I let him sit me there. Then he went back to my car and drove it onto the parking lot behind me. Now LA's "beautiful people" could get home in time for their favorite talk show, or "do weekday brunch" with some jerk who really will get their stupid-shit movie made, or arrive late to work with a wonderful tale about the freak who blocked traffic so he could weep hysterically in the middle of Barrington and Pico, the dumb fuck. Looking back, I can see where, even as I crashed and burned I was realizing what was going on around me...albeit in the vaguest, most generic way. And I felt vile for doing it.

I think that's what brought me back. The simple act of walking had loosened insanity's grip on my feeble brain, but it was the understanding I had that what was happening to me meant shit to everybody else that bounced away the sense of total guilt and injustice I was feeling – because it fucking irritated me. How dare people not care that someone they don't know is suffering? What kind of animals were they? That cute little voice in the back of my head that always pops up at the worst times laughed, "They're human, you dumb shit, and you did it, too." Yeah, and isn't that just how it goes?

At that moment, I found a path back to control. I fought my way out of the whiteness, step by horrible step until I was able to look up and hear the cars screaming past and see lights changing from red to green to red again and smell the thick odor of gasoline wafting from a nearby service station. I kept tiptoeing right up to the edge of toppling over the cliff into convulsive sobs but somehow – I still don't know how – I kept from taking that final step.

Then I noticed someone was beside me, sitting in my car and waiting for me to acknowledge...him...her...I couldn't tell, right then). I was sick, ready to vomit, and my eyes were so out of focus, I couldn't even make out what color his clothing was. But that didn't matter. Whoever it was waited until they knew I was back with the living, then they squatted beside me, put a hand on my back and asked, "You okay, now?"

I could only nod, in answer.

"Can you tell me what happened?"

The best I could force myself to whisper was, "He's dead."

"I'm sorry. A relative?" I shook my head. "A friend?"

157

I shook my head. He must have really been confused by now. I was aware enough by this point to offer more, even if it only added to his confusion. I mouthed two words. Croaked them. Whispered them. Something. "Bobby Carapisi."

It was clear enough for my watcher to say, "Oh. I heard about that. Did you know him?"

"No."

"He wasn't a friend of yours?"

"No," I barely sighed. Then I took a deep breath and added, "Fellow victim."

He rose at hearing that. "Fellow? Oh. Are you – uh, you the other guy?" I nodded. "That's rough."

I almost began to cry, again. I looked at the guy – hell, I think it was a guy (my eyes were still bleary from the tears) but I couldn't have told you if he was. Or if he was black, white, pink or purple, right then. How old he was. Even if he was really looking at me with kindness. All I knew was, he had just said the first truly decent thing to me that I had heard since all this mess began. He had acknowledged my pain without anything in the way of an adjective or accusation, and I loved him for it. Absolutely. Positively. Without reservation. I wanted to build a shrine to this man. I wanted to have the pope elevate him to saint, whether he was Catholic or not. I wanted to shout to the world that there still were real honest-to-God-decent human beings in this so-called City of Angels, and I knew there was a special place in heaven for him.

All I wound up saying was, "Yeah."

"You gonna be okay, now?"

I nodded...which surprised me. I didn't know that. Not for sure. But when he asked, it seemed to be the most natural response, and I really meant it. At least, I really meant to try and be.

"Wait a while before you drive. Traffic's brutal."

"What d'you expect from LA, man?" I responded, and I cast him a pathetic smile.

158

"No shit." Then he strolled away.

I don't know if he got in a car or hopped on a bus or if he walked into a nearby store. My eyes were just barely back to being sort of usable, and there were people all around, ignoring me as best they could. So all that happened was he just...sort of wandered away, like what he had done was completely and totally common and natural. That it wasn't made what happened even more exquisite. The fact that one human being had taken whatever time was necessary to help a fellow human being keep from getting lost forever sparked more hope in me than any relative or religion or lover has ever been able to do. I mean, he brought me back to God.

Now don't get me wrong, here – like I said at the start of this story, I'll never be some religious freak pounding the Bible with one hand and yelling "Repent" with the other. I still view all organized religions as being nothing more than slave-makers, where the better slave you are to their version of God, the more they promise you forever-after. And the more they insist you hate all the other slaves, who are also being promised forever-after. It doesn't matter if you call your God Yahweh or Buddah or Krishna, or if you follow Jesus or Mohammed or the fuckin' Pope! What matters is you think for yourselves on the subject. I've never accepted the idea that God wants weak-willed androids programmed to spout little catch-phrases by rote; He knows the men on earth will tell them lies about what to believe and what to think and what to say and what to do so they can control them and build their own pathetic little empires of televangelism and cause explosions of vicious jihad and expand upon their feelings of serene superiority. God wants men to stop. To question. To say, "Wait a minute, that's not the way I understood it and I don't care how much you say you know!" God wants men who will do right by others, spread love and understanding, accept and tolerate other opinions because they aren't necessarily wrong just because they are different. I'd stepped away from him because I was confusing the message with the obnoxious messenger. I'd now been lead back by this simple act of kindness.

As for my hysterics, twenty-twenty hindsight shows me just how close I was to doing exactly what Bobby did. I was wound so tight, I couldn't see it; but by him doing it first, I had recognized just how futile it was. No one really cared. He was nothing more some over-priced jock who couldn't handle the pressure. Look at the drug problems some of them have – and the stories of women abused and the guys who're tossed off the field due to injury or simple age. Those stories are a dime a dozen. And if I'd followed suit, I'd have been even less important.

And that pissed me off. Really fuckin' pissed me off. At Allen. At that stupid-shit cunt of an A-D-A. At the media, in general. It was insane, how furious I got.

The first surge came as I finally got in my car and pulled onto Barrington, going north. I began muttering "those fucks" over and over to keep from weeping and then to keep from turning my car around and driving down to the criminal courts building and ripping Ionescue's throat out. I began fantasizing about what I'd do to her and to Lewis, the defense attorney, and Grant. And especially to Allen.

Oh, his got really creative in the torture area. I'd read this old "French bible" once, about some Frenchmen who go to spy for the Russians against Japan in 1904. They were caught and executed in some intensely graphic ways. My "favorite" was when one guy was tied to a chair then had an iron spike driven up his ass. Then another and another until the first one burst through his throat or tore into his brain. Another spy was stripped naked, lashed to a stretcher and carried past two rows of a thousand men, each of them beating him with a bamboo cane until he was nothing but raw bloody flesh. Of course, both men shot their wads as they died (it was a sex novel, not reality). Then I remembered Allen had done that same thing to me, practically, which killed that moment of pleasure-planning. Mother-fucker probably got off on that shit.

So I shifted into even nastier ways to get even. All of them were the goriest and vilest things I could imagine, none of them the least bit sensual, even for a sick freak like little Allen. I was going to peel his skin away with a razor blade, by the square inch, starting with his dick. I was going to shove a plastic bag over his head, with two pin-pricks of air to seep in and let him slowly gasp for breath till his brain gave out. I was going to blind him with acid and sear his throat with lime and shove a salt enema into his bowels, all at the same time. Oh, I poured over the ideas like a madman plotting the end of the world in a James Bond flick, not knowing where I was driving or caring how insane I must have seemed to passing motorists.

And then I stopped.

I was on Santa Monica and Second, a block from the ocean, waiting for a red light. A haze had settled over the bay, letting the water sort of dissolve into the grey sky as a gentle mist pushed what little heat there was away. Crowds passed from one corner to the next, tourists from God knows where and clerks from the Promenade and brokers from the garden offices and the muttering homeless who went back and forth to nowhere. I smelled Indian food and bar-b-cue and fish and chips and fresh coffee. My anger drifted away with the aromas. I looked to my right. Don't know why; I just did. And I saw it.

At the base of the parking garage halfway down the block was a small pile of flowers, almost exactly between the two round middle-sized trees that stood silently in the sidewalk. They surrounded a sad little make-shift cross that had been propped against the concrete, and people were slowing as they passed by. Some of them stopped. Some of them shook their heads. Some of them shrugged to each other in confusion. The sidewalk was clean. The trees were undamaged. And I knew this is where it happened.

I turned and parked in a red zone (fuck the ticket) and slipped over to the little shrine. I now saw there was a full array of roses and carnations and gladiolas and mums and lilies, some wrapped in brown paper, some in tissue, some with nothing but a blue or pink or red ribbon tied around the stem. Baby's breath and ferns and streaks of colored reeds mingled in the fray, as did cards and shreds of paper and bits of cardboard holding some sentiment or another. I kneeled beside this tiny shrine and began to read expression after expression of sorrow that so young a life had been crushed by so terrible a burden.

And then I read a note that said, "I understand."

Those two words sent a shock through me. I found another one that read, "I'm so sorry. I should have said something." It was signed Timmy. A third card read, "You showed me I am not alone. God be with you. Carlos."

I suddenly began to wonder, could others really have been through the same thing as Bobby and me? Could Allen have been that prolific? Or were other men in the same boat – getting raped by a guy and having no one believe them? Having people belittle their trauma? Having no one to turn to?

I jumped back to my car (two seconds before a parking freak rolled up) and drove it into the parking garage. Then I crossed the street to stand in front of a theater and watch the little shrine as it slowly grew. Most of the people bearing flowers were women (something I learned about baseball is it has some very devoted female fans) but every now and then, a man would come up, lay his flower on the dirt then walk away. Still the majority of those were older and they rarely had a card.

But through the course of the afternoon, I saw five more guys under the age of thirty leave notes that said things like, "I wish we could have talked" and "I was in your shoes" and "God understands. He has to." One was African-American; another was Latino. Two could have been cowboys from some Midwestern state, they way they dressed; and they were only ten minutes apart. I would have sat there and kept watching the shrine build, even as it was drifting into twilight, but the last one...the last one looked a little bit like Bobby and me – dark hair, good shape, mid-twenties, sturdy build but with a thin goatee – and he snapped me to attention.

He looked like one of those fraternity guys I hated so much in college – blue linen shirt tucked into cargo shorts, topsiders on sockless feet – but the second I saw him, I knew we had at least one connection. When he walked away, I slipped over to read what I think was his card – "I should of called the cops, man. Wish I had. I'm sorry." And that cinched it.

I followed him. I don't know why; I just felt the need to see what happened next with him. He walked down to Arizona and back up to the Promenade, where he met a beautiful girl. I heard him say, "That bathroom was disgusting," as they merged into the dinner crowd. His attitude was that of a guy who'd just popped off to take a piss, not be in solidarity with one of society's latest victims.

But then just before he vanished, he glanced back and looked directly at me, as if he'd noticed I was his new shadow. His dark eyes grew haunted; his lips hinted at a grimace behind their smile. He planned to keep hiding what had happened to him. Like Bobby had.

Like others had. Like I had, really, from myself. And he'd grow old with the memory and drink too much and probably get divorced and second-guess himself the rest of his life, and the knowledge of that sliced into my heart. I raised my hand, not in a wave but as if to say, "I understand, too." His lips twitched, then he looked away and was swallowed by the crowd. I think he saw and understood. I hope he did.

I wandered back to the garage. Drifted, really, like a raft on the Mississippi gliding past a dark unthinking world. I carried no conscious thoughts to be remembered...except for a simple painful understanding that built from deep within – people cared about Bobby. If it had been me who jumped from that garage, there would have been no flowers, no cards, no mourners passing by. No one would have quaked with grief and anger. No one would have told my story, or wept at the injustice, or screamed at God over the death of a man they did not know. I would have vanished into the nothingness that surrounds our existence. Been lost in the white endless quiet that enveloped me earlier that day, erased from the memory of my family. And my friends. And even the law that claims it's there to protect me. And not one person would have noticed or cared. And oh, God, how I hated Bobby for having that.

Admitting this makes me ill. Even now. Just reading the line on my computer causes my brain to stop and my stomach to shiver and a voice within demand I find some excuse or more decent explanation for why I felt something so irrational and vile. And that only adds to my sense of selfishness. I know it's a cliché to claim that we are callous animals whose worlds revolve around ourselves, and how we cannot truly appreciate the suffering of others (except in the abstract) but can easily demand our own complaints become deeply personal for all. And I also know, now that I've had time to digest my actions and reactions and recognize that I didn't really hate Bobby but only hated the realization that no one in general cared about me as much as they did him. But it's still just a back-assed attempt at avoiding the one true aspect to my feelings at that moment – I had just helped drive a man to his death...and I envied him for it. Talk about a disconnect from reality.

The shrine had grown a bit since I left. A skinny teenage Goth kid was detaching a nose ring when I rounded the corner. He set it in one of the Calla Lillies then glared at me as if to scream, "Don't you

163

fuckin' notice that!" In respect, I looked away. He walked up to and past me, all attitude in black everything. I just sighed, got my car and drove home.

I sat in my apartment, held Jag in my lap and watched CNN and its ongoing rehash of Bobby's suicide. One of their "star" sports guys waxed eloquently about what a wonderful baseball player he had been. Never mind the snide comments he'd made on air just last week. Never mind how he'd hinted that Bobby was probably lying about the assault, that he'd just been caught fooling around on his wife, and with a guy, of all things! Never mind that he all but said Bobby should quit because he had disgraced the game. Now Bobby was always going to be "Mr. Delivery" to him, a hint of misty-eyed feeling in his throat as he said it. I flicked over to ESPN. Same kind of shit. I'd have puked if I'd been feeling anything.

I began flipping channels. MSNBC and ABC and NBC and CBS and all of the rest kept saying the same basic thing, over and over and over, "How sad that this great young ball player is gone, and isn't it horrible what the fans did to him, along with the tabloid press, while we, alone, stood by him through it all?" Step by step, you could see them distancing themselves from having been responsible for Bobby's death in any way, form or fashion. Fox News Network, which had been the nastiest about him, quickly reached the point where he was yesterday's info, worthy only of a quick blurb buried in the sports recap, all within the space of twenty-four hours.

Then came word of the retaliations. Vicious assaults on gay men in Chicago, Boston, Nashville, Miami, Houston, even a few in supposedly decadent L-A. One guy in Phoenix was shot because a carload of vatos just thought he was queer. Turned out he had a wife, three kids and a girlfriend on the side (not that that means anything). But they were still just "twenty-five-words-or-less" blurbs on Fox and CNN. Then one moron with a single-digit intelligence quotient tossed a Molotov cocktail into an Atlanta gay bar and burned three men to death. Even that only bumped the story up to "fifty-words-or-less" until it turned out the men were African-American and the Atlanta PD agreed to treat it as a hate crime; that way they could focus on the race aspect and not face the fact that America, rather than blame itself for its hideous behavior, was finding a convenient scapegoat. The new and improved sacrificial lamb.

My phone rang. I ignored it. Unplugged it, again. And turned off my cell to keep from chancing any contact, at all. I knew it was only a matter of time before the pundits would take over and remind people of my part in this mess. Fortunately, my number was unpublished, I'd never given out my address and my apartment was in the back of the building so no one could peek in, should they ever be able to track me down. But just in case, I plugged my headphones into the TV to watch and listen as the bastards in suits with the absolute certainty of their opinions started in and they did not disappoint.

One televangelist said, "Of course, it's all the fault of American's leniency with the homosexuals. Liberals makin' it seem like it's fine to rape good heterosexual boys and turn them into one of their acolytes." He was what even Grandmother would have called, "too stupid to know he's stupid."

And there was Ian, yakking on "The Gary Phillips" show about how American's intolerance of being gay is what really drove Bobby to his death. "If he'd been allowed to be a gay man and do as he pleased, he'd be alive today." Still swearing Bobby was a closet case. The dumb fuck.

166

The rest were too fucking typical for words. "It's the Democrats' fault." "It's the Republicans' fault." "It's God's fault." "It's the atheists' fault." "It's the femi-nazis' fault." "It's men's fault." "It's everybody's but my fault." And on and on and on, ad nauseum.

Still, it took four more days for the story to jump into the headlines, again. Some of those demon fag-haters from Wichita, Kansas drove all the way to Philadelphia to picket the funeral home where Bobby was on view. They had their usual signs reading, "God Says Kill Fags" and "Bobby Carapese (SIC) Burns in Hell" and "God Rejoiced at Bobby's Death" and filth like that. I think they figured they'd get their picketing done and their picture in the news and then toodle on home thinking they'd provided a great service to the devil they worshiped. What I don't think they expected was just how pissed off Bobby's family would get. And just how big that family was.

Soon as they arrived at the funeral parlor and pulled out their signs, two of Bobby's brothers went over. One of them was caught on a paparazzi's tape saying, "If my mother sees one of those f***n' signs, I'm rippin' your f***n' head out your f***n' ass, you f***n' got me?" The only reason he didn't do it then was a cop stepped in and promised he'd keep the demons a good distance, away. Which would be hard, seeing as how the street was only about twenty-five feet wide.

By this time, the news crews were gathering, hoping for a good fight to use as a lead into the Six O'Clock News. I'm sure they were aiming for something like, "Carapisi Family Fights Protestors at Funeral! Four arrested." What they got was better – for them, anyway.

The presence of broadcast news cameras always adds to the attitude of scum like the Wichita demons. And as if on cue, they began yelling and chanting the second anyone looked like they were recording them, causing people who were arriving for the viewing to look over in disgust. One or two even called back, "That's NOT what Jesus would do!" As if the devil gives a damn about the Son of God and His teachings.

It was when Bobby's father arrived with two of his sisters and an elderly aunt that things began to get scary. Apparently, they thought the old woman was Bobby's grandmother, because they began yelling, "Your grandson burns in Hell!" and "God laughs at your loss! Rejoice with him!" That's when he and about two dozen men – brothers, sons, nephews, buddies, co-workers – suddenly barreled over and surrounded the Wichita demons. Completely. Every one of them at least two-hundred pounds of solid beef and all of them focused on that slime. It looked beautiful on the news, almost like a scene staged by Eisenstein or Lang, with this sudden rush of black-coated men crossing a wet narrow street to envelope a rag-tag group of nobodies in their darkness.

The men just stood there, saying nothing but sending howling messages with the daggers in their eyes. Bobby's father is reputed to have told them, "You got two choices – you go to hell, or you go the fuck home. It's up to you," but none of the news cameras caught it on tape. Whatever he said, the men just kept standing there until the demons put away their signs and got back in their mini-vans and drove away like dogs with their tails stuck between their legs. Then the pool of black coats funneled into the funeral home.

The commentators loved it. They praised the actions of Bobby's family and friends to no end, going on and on about how the best way to deal with a situation like that was exactly like they did – no violence, just a quiet show of overwhelming force and willingness to back it up. I nearly broke my TV throwing a half-full can of soda at it.

I mean, where were those guys when Bobby needed them most? After the story broke and he could have really used their help? Where was their "quiet show of overwhelming force" when he was still alive and being ripped to shreds? Why didn't they put that line of black-coated men between him and the world of baseball – hell, the whole fucking world – before he died? How dare anyone praise them for finally doing what they should have done from the beginning?

Not once while Bobby was crashing towards oblivion did any of them openly raise a hand to slow his descent. His brothers and sisters and cousins and in-laws and buddies were brutally silent. No one went to his home to try and save him, no one but his mother and aunt. Which showed that his family was at least aware of his situation, yet not one of his brothers or sisters, not one of his teammates, not one of his friends reached out to him like Gerrod had to me. What? Were they waiting for HIM to say something? Did they not really understand what was going on with him? Did they believe the crap in the papers and on the TV and radio that maybe, just maybe, he really was a closet case who got caught out and was causing the family embarrassment? That maybe he was asking for what happened to him? That if they showed him any sympathy, they'd be painted with the pink brush, as well? I don't know. They won't talk to me. Not one of them. The only one who even said anything more than fuck off was his brother, Rich, who snarled, "I ain't talkin' to the cocksucker who helped kill my brother."

Of course he's right; I did help kill Bobby. And I am deeply ashamed of that. But he conveniently forgets he never even tried to save Bobby. Never called him to say he'd be okay. Never made a single solitary step to offer his younger brother a hand. And their mother told me she tore into Rich over it. Rich and Tony and all the rest. She has yet to forgive them.

The only person I know of who stood up for Bobby at the height of the chaos was Scott, the catcher for Cincinnati, who got blistered in the press for demanding a trade because he didn't want to work for a town whose people were such animals. He fired right back, calling a couple of sportscasters some choice names on air...and got fined by the Baseball Commission for it (the fines were quietly waived after Bobby's suicide; sort of a low-key acknowledgement that Scott was right and they were assholes). Everyone else turned quiet on him, just as viciously quiet as the rest of the world, just when he needed their support most. Yet here they were being praised for finally reacting to the worst of the worst. It made me sick. And so fucking angry, I had to turn the TV off before I threw it through a window...all at the top of my voice.

That's when Jag whimpered at me. Apparently I WAS at the top of my voice. I crashed to my knees to hug him. "It's gonna be okay, buddy. It's gonna be okay." That's when I finally looked around and noticed more than a week had passed from the last time I'd paid life any attention. Cartons of nuked food were lying everywhere along with devastated cans of beans and soup and whatever else I'd had in the cupboards or fridge. Empty soda cans clinked underfoot. Filthy dishes were stacked everywhere. The windows were closed and the blinds were drawn and it seemed like midnight, but it was seven-twenty a.m. I don't think I'd showered or changed my clothes since the day Bobby died, but it wasn't like before, just after my rape; it was more like I just didn't notice how much time had passed. The place smelled. Shit, I smelled and I was surprised to realize I was finally back to where I could give a damn about such crap. I opened the windows, found a fan and started to air my pigsty out...then set to cleaning it up.

The simple act of picking up trash helped me shift my focus back to reality. What I was doing wasn't being trendily weary, nor was I happily drifting on a cloud of incoherence for all that time, gallantly allowing my mind a chance to heal in preparation for the rest of my life. The fact is, while watching the news I kept reliving everything that had happened over and over and over in a crazy hope that if I did it often enough, the outcome would change. If not for real, at least in my own head. I understand that's a sign of insanity. That may well be true, but the fact was I could not honestly (and coherently) face the honest to God truth as regards my part in this disaster. Not just yet.

I finished filling my second Hefty bag and went to a window to see how the garbage looked, like I'd done so many times in the last couple of months for no particular reason. Funny thing is, for the first time the bin was empty. Nothing but leftover smudge to see. I carried both bags down the stairs and dumped them in then looked up just in time to make the trip worthwhile.

It was overcast and cool. A hint of winter rain was in the air. An almost breeze was tickling the tree just to my right. And a hummingbird danced past to play in the flowers on the bush to my left. I watched as he whirred and darted and checked out the buds and dipped in for a sip (at least, I think it was a he). His wings were almost invisible, they moved so fast, and he was a lovely combination of dark neon green and bright neon red, with hints of purple, blue and gold glimmering through and eyes like little black pearls. So tiny. So fragile. So busy with his life. So heartbreakingly beautiful. Then he stopped. He perched on a branch, breathing heavily, and looked back at me as if to ask, "What you lookin' at, bub?" I grinned, still without thinking, and went back to my apartment.

I peeled off my shirt and jeans and everything and set the shower to going as hot as I could stand it. I let the water roll over my face and 'cross my shoulders and down my back and stomach and legs. Then I leaned back against the side of the stall and let the steam rise and fill my lungs and heart and soul. I didn't zone in there, though; deep down

I knew the hot water would soon end and I'd have to finish in cold if I took too long. I absently began to lather up. Slowly, almost carefully, I cleaned every part of my body I could get to. I flashed back to the day after my encounter with Allen and the shower I never took after Doctor Finnerman and the SANE and nurse Pavel and Grant and Iglesias and my deep desperate need for the oblivion of sleep and everything else were done with me. I vaguely recognized the sense of non-urgent-urgency I'd had since that day was gone. I could simply luxuriate in the cleanliness of the soap. The beauty of the shimmer it left on my skin. The scent of it taking me back to a day before I'd been tainted. I shampooed, rinsed, repeated the actions, all by rote. And yet, not. This wasn't like the time when Moritz had told me to bathe. This was just...well, it just felt nice. Wonderful. I finished the moment the water turned tepid. Perfect timing, for once.

I stepped out and wiped the condensation from the glass and looked at myself through the pattern of streaks and drops left behind. And I flashed back to that hotel room only two (three? four?) months prior and realized that was the last time I had seen myself in a mirror. Comparatively speaking, I looked neither better nor worse. It was like I'd gone into a holding pattern, waiting for clearance to continue my slide into hell or whatever fate I would allow for myself. But this time I could see more than just the deep disgusting differences in my psyche. My eyes were still hollow instead of bright, but they were also cold. My skin was pasty instead of rose hued, despite the hot shower, and it too was cold. I'd lost a few more pounds and it showed in how much deeper my cheeks sank. It was me at fifty before I was half that age. It was pathetic.

I ran some lukewarm water into the sink and shaved, something I'd never done naked before. I know it's an odd thing to think about, but the thought simply came as a "never did that before" jog from my memory. I gently dried off with my one semi-clean towel, rolled some deodorant under my arms and strolled over to the closet.

I didn't own a chest of drawers; all my underwear and socks and sweaters and foldable items of clothing were laid on a shelving unit shoved into one corner. I picked out a pair of briefs, a white t-shirt and pair of black socks and pulled them on, right there...something else I never did. Then I took the only clothes I had left on hangers – a white cotton shirt and that long forgotten pair of torn black Dockers – and slipped into those. The pants were loose, so I cinched the belt a notch tighter. Two notches. Doing that helped hide the damage to the material enough to where if you weren't looking for it, you'd never see it. I found my black shoes (the ones that were always tied) and shoved my feet into them, then I looked at myself in the full-length mirror. I still had not one bit of thought or emotion at seeing this "crystal-chic" type freak staring back.

I got my wallet, got my car keys, gave Jag a pat on the head and left.

My Volvo started up on the first try and I pulled away. I still had zero idea of where I was going or what I was doing. I just drove. East down Pico. Under the 405. Past Westside Pavilion. Over the tiny hill by Beverly Glen. Straight to Fairfax. Left toward the Hills. Passing Ethiopian and Jewish shops and restaurants, then passing the museums and Farmer's Market and the humongous Grove shopping center and CBS and Canter's up to Melrose. Then right to head down the strip.

The high school was busy. Traffic had yet to be jammed with the lunchtime crush. Meters were open everywhere. I stopped at one, plunked in a quarter and walked along. There were a few tourists looking around with disappointment at how sedate Melrose seemed, even with its wall murals and occasional head shops. "It just ain't like Haight-Ashbury, Oliver, that's fer dang sure."

I turned down a side street and turned, again, to head down the alley. And two doors down stood Rene's thirty year-old Mercedes carefully parked in one of the two parking slots. The aroma of his lunch preparation danced up to greet me like it was overjoyed to see the prodigal son.

"So this is where I'm going," I thought as I wandered up to the door.

I looked in...and there was Rene, unchanged, dipping his finger into a pot to test the sauce. Steam swirled around him and tickled through the silver hair that still flew out from under his chef's cap. He wasn't happy with what he found, so he grabbed a pinch of this and a dab of that to fling into the pot. Then he stirred the sauce. And saw me. His expression did not change, nor did he hesitate in his stirring; he just glanced me over.

I gulped, my mind a blank, my mouth dry. But then words began popping out, soft, croaking, whispers of, "I'm sorry. I left you in a bad spot. No excuse. I'm so sorry."

He checked another pot, still casting little glances at me. It needed a dash more salt.

I kept babbling. "I'm going out to get another job. If I can. I think I'm pretty good at waiting tables. I – I was hoping I could – well, could I give you as a reference? I know it's asking a lot – but I need to – to..."

Rene motioned me in; I entered. He pointed me to his ratty little table covered with paperwork and such; I sat in the one chair. He pulled down a plate, put some Ravioli Caruso on it and set it before me; I stared at it. Silverware wrapped in a tacky red napkin appeared by my right hand; I looked up at him.

"Rene..."

"Eat," was all he said, then he turned back to his pots.

I ate. Slowly. Tasting every bite. Loving it. No, luxuriating in it. The warmth of it drifted into my stomach and gently spread into my heart then through my whole body. Oh, sweet Jesus, it was Heaven, purest Heaven. I licked the plate clean, and I mean that literally.

When I was done, Rene appeared by my side, again. "I can use you Tuesday, Thursday lunch, Friday, Sunday night."

I felt like I'd been slapped with cold water. Did he say what I thought he said? "Here? But I – I – didn't..."

"Can you work lunch, today?"

"Yes."

"I need a host. We have a big party coming. You park on the street?"

"Meter."

"Put it by my car. This time only. Then prep the tables. Laila is alone until noon. Again."

He turned back to his pots. I couldn't move. I was afraid that if I did, I'd see nothing but my dreary four walls instead of these happy steaming pots and hear my pissy neighbors instead of the plinks and plops of Rene's cuisine nearing perfection and smell the cabbage crap Mrs. Vanden was cooking instead of the insanely gorgeous aromas combining in this tiny kitchen. Then Rene looked at me and gave me an irritated flip of his hand to tell me to go. I went.

I ran back to my car, parked it beside his Mercedes, and got to work prepping the tables. I smoothed the beautifully tacky covers, making them hang just right. Then I changed all the old candles. Then I neatened up the silly little plastic flowers. Then I made sure every place that needed it had plates and silverware and glasses (and there were a LOT of them; who DID set up last night?). Then I got to rolling fresh silverware for later. And finally Laila zoomed in, shivering in her usual huff.

"You cannot beLIEVE the fuckin' idiots on the – !" and her voice slammed shut at seeing me.

I cast her a weak little smile, said something dumb like, "Hi, I'm Eric; I'll be your backup, today," and kept rolling.

Laila walked in a circle around me, stunned into silence (the one and only time in her life, probably), and slipped into the kitchen. I finally heard her say, "Rene?"

"What!?"

I snuck a peek to see how she was going to react (nervous for the first time) and I saw her just stand there, for a moment, then glance at me. She was weeping. Oh, thank God; that meant she wasn't pissed at me, anymore. Then she kissed Rene on the cheek (to his intense irritation) and came out to open the place for lunch.

I still work at "Il Senso." And anytime Rene needs someone to cover, anytime he's short or over-staffed, anytime he needs backup in the kitchen instead of a waiter, I do what's necessary, no problem. The hostess don't show? I take over without a word, even though it means turning fewer tables. He needs the place cleaned? I do it for nothing. If he throws a fit or screams at one of the other waiters, I smooth things over. I've even washed and waxed and polished his old Mercedes and fixed some little problems it has, all at no charge. It's the least I can do. He gave me back my future.

Life slowly reduced itself to a semi-gentle flow over the next few months. On the outside, anyway. I got back to working six or seven shifts a week and making money enough to rebuild my existence. I started back to the gym after a month to regain more of what I considered normalcy. As for Bobby's death, the pundits' screams, sportsmen's comments and religious tirades barked at the press and their congregations by Satan's attack dogs became a part of history within three weeks. It almost seemed as if peace was at hand.

Gerrod even showed up on my doorstep, one day, just I was getting home from work. Seems the news had permeated into my family's existence and they'd been trying to get hold of me. For weeks. Mom had even been fielding phone calls from reporters of all persuasions asking how she felt about my being the reason Bobby killed himself. She'd told them they were nuts to think that, but she wanted to hear what was going on directly from me. So I called her and, as Gerrod listened in, filled her in on everything. Absolutely everything. By the time I was done, Gerrod was white as a sheet, and considering how tan he usually is, that was some feat.

"Christ, Eric," he said, "you could've let us know."

Mom heard him. "He's right, dear. We'd have backed you up, completely."

"Yeah," was all I could say. I mean, I knew that. They'd always supported me. No matter how much of an idiot I was – and there were occasions...well, there were occasions where they had to. So I had no honest response to their comments. And I could read the hurt in Gerrod's eyes that I hadn't trusted them.

Like Bobby hadn't trusted his family, I thought. But he had reason not to. I finally saw that. He knew, deep down, it would have made things worse, somehow. How, I couldn't fathom till later; I just had my first glimmer of the idea.

Gerrod shook his head and looked at me. "Is there anything we can do for you?"

I just shook my head. Then pulled him close and held him. No tears. No sobs. Just held him. And he took the phone, told mom, "We'll call you back," and held me just as tight.

Dad arrived, a couple days later, and straightened out a few things with Ionescue and Grant. Filed a claim for victims' reimbursement and saw to it I began seeing a therapist, again.

"I'm paying for it, Eric, whether you go or not. So you damn well better go."

I went, but it was to one of my own choosing – Moritz's friend, Lucia. She was perfect for me. Calm when I got tense. Patient when I got quiet. Soothing when I wept. Willing to hold me when I needed it.

And I did need it. Because the only factor not joining in with the soft new world around me was my own turmoil, my own guilt over what happened. That actually seemed to struggle against becoming a fragile stream. Actually seemed to fight to keep its raging torrent of emotional ups and downs.

I might spend a few days thinking things were going well enough, life is livable and maybe I really can start over, but then something would snap at me like a sharp wet towel and within hours I'd be beating myself up over every stupid thing I'd ever done in my short stupid life and using each and every detail all to prove to myself how worthless I was, with Bobby's suicide being the capper. It became a nice little loop of recurring events, where I'd swoop so low I'd contemplate ending it all just to get a little peace from my self-flagellation. But something would keep me from taking that final absolute step, some wall standing solid between me and oblivion (what it was and why it was there, I still don't know), and I'd wind up calling Lucia to get convinced that things weren't worth dying over, not just yet. Then I'd feel better for a few days more...until something smashed my hated version of reality back to the foreground of my existence and sent me careening into the whole thing, again.

It happened often enough to where I could recognize its ignition point and time my actions. "Uh-oh, this guy looks a lot like Bobby. Oh, shit. Okay...it'll now be three hours and twenty-seven minutes to when I begin ripping myself to shreds. Should I call and make an appointment with Lucia now or just wait for the usual pattern to fulfill itself?" I usually waited. It seemed appropriate, considering my sense of guilt and my ridiculous insistence on repeating myself, over and over.

But after a while, as with anything emotionally draining, the episodes became less and less frequent. They still lay in wait, ready to pounce at a moment's notice, but the three days respite quietly expanded into a week's respite, and finally the fact that I hadn't done the crash and burn in almost three weeks lulled me into a premature belief that I had finally achieved some sort of mental balance. Needless to say, I wasn't exactly correct, as I was shown seven months after Bobby's death.

Hmph. I just realized that's how I measure things now. There was my life Before Bobby's Death, and everything that occurred After Bobby's Death. I still have sudden realizations like that. And now I can see that his destruction means more to me than the idea of AD and BC. Whether we're on a Julian calendar or Octavian or dating existence in thousands of years instead of millions or billions. Like America before 9/11 and after. There's this sharp thick curtain of time descended between the two eras, which makes one seem to be centuries ago, even though it was only a few months. Writing this book shows me just how easily I can be...shit, shows me just how easily I can let myself be distracted by nonsense.

Back to my point.

"Il Senso" was busy that night. Not too intense, but I was glad for the work. Gerrod's wedding date had been set, and I had less than two months to pull together enough money to pay my own way there (I was finally getting back to my "independent to a fault" stage). I'd already turned six tables when, just before eight, a woman who looked familiar entered with a guy I would like to have become familiar with (if I ever decided to allow that part of life's flow back in). She noticed me but didn't seem to know me, so I decided she was probably someone who'd eaten there before and her face just registered in my brain, for some reason. Maybe she'd been with another good-looker I'd have been interested in, once upon a time...which would've surprised me. She didn't seem like the sort who goes for (or gets) hot male model/soap opera star hunks all that often. If ever. She had too much of a low-key deer-caught-in-the-headlights feel to her. Didn't matter; Wilda, our all-too-erratic hostess, sat her at one of Laila's tables, and the woman paid me no attention.

I didn't pay her any, either. Until I was exiting the kitchen with a tray holding a split of champagne and two fluted glasses and almost ran her down as she headed for the ladies' room. I apologized and she looked at me and smiled with recognition, but in a hurt way that slammed her eyes into me and I finally knew who she was – Ms. Calvert. Wilson-mother-fucking-Lewis' witness in that hotel room, so many centuries ago. I stopped dead.

She continued on, not even giving me a second glance, but I spun into a quick-flash recap of that meeting, his nastiness, my turmoil, the DVD, my elation after the revelations it brought about...and its tragic consequences, and I started to shake. No, quake from the inside out. We're talking 8.6 here. And somewhere in the back on my mind, my sense of timing as regards my next emotional near-annihilation kicked in, and I knew this one'd be a doozie, as Gramma'd say. Two hours and eleven minutes to meltdown. Which would put it almost exactly at the time I was prepping the restaurant for tomorrow. Oh, God – not the best time for that to happen.

The next thing I knew, I was in the kitchen. I must have backed in without thinking. The tray was still on my hand, perfectly balanced, but I could not remember who it went to. I couldn't move. Period. The paranoid side of my brain was kicking into overtime. Why'd she come here? Why'd she smile at me in recognition? Why'd she ignore me if she recognized me? Was it just a coincidence? Just one of those L-A flukes where you meet someone you once knew in high school who's lived in L-A for years in an apartment just four blocks from yours (which actually happened to me, once)? But Lewis knew I worked here, so she must know, too. And she'd entered with a guy who was so gorgeous that, since she knew I was gay then she'd also be pretty damned sure I'd notice him. And then I'd be sure to notice her. And I mean, her date was so fuckin' hot any gay man'd be aware of him, no matter what he was into. And then, thinking about it, I noticed she and her guy didn't act much like lovers or a married couple or even two people on a blind date. They seemed more like brother and sister. Looked more like brother and sister. More and more like brother and sister, once the thought hit my speeding imagination. Which probably meant this was deliberate on her part. So why? Why? Why? Why?

I caught a glimpse of Rene looking at me, irritated and probably about to launch into a screaming fit, but then Laila roared in, crying, "Dots in sauce and vodka." Then she looked at me and, as if reading my mind, added, "Table five's been looking for that."

Okay, do or die time, Eric. You have just over two hours to get ready for your latest bout of masochism; till then, you can hide in the kitchen and shake with anticipation or do your job and not let Laila and Rene down, again. Let them down, again? After what they'd done for me? I'd rather slit my throat. So...tray still balanced on one hand, I jammed the other one into the ice-maker. The feel of frozen water crushing my fingers and jamming hard against my skin broke my tailspin long enough for me to take a deep breath, straighten my back, wipe my forehead with that cold clammy hand and head on into the dining area.

I served the split to a very nice middle-aged couple from Nashville who knew people in Albert Lea, an oversized farm town south of Minneapolis. A pleasant chat was had by all (though I cannot remember one word of it) as I popped the bottle and filled their glasses. And when I served their dinner a few minutes later – Ravioli Caruso for both – they complimented Rene on his most excellent sauce. All so very nice.

I also checked on my other tables, took orders from new diners, gave Wilda her fourteenth smoke break and basically treated the whole evening not as my regular job but as if I was portraying a waiter in a movie. It wasn't the world's greatest performance, but it got me through the night and kept me from paying any further attention to Ms. Calvert et fils...if he was her brother. I couldn't tell you for certain when they left; I only noticed that a single woman was seated at their table just after nine-thirty.

My last customers left at ten-thirty-four, this being a Tuesday night (and don't you think I didn't work THAT little detail into my paranoid fantasies). Laila followed them five minutes later. I now had twenty-one minutes to blast-off. If I worked fast, I could have everything done and be in my car and on the cell phone before it hit, full force; I had Lucia's number at the top of my list, and in the privacy of my little Volvo I could do and say anything I damned well pleased or needed to.

I was out of that joint in nineteen minutes, flat (a record for me). My car was just over a block away. I ran, already starting to gasp for breath (and let me emphasize, it was not from that tiny little jog; I'd already been running a bit to get back into shape), and the quaking was back.

I reached my Volvo, slammed inside, had my phone out and was fighting back the first white-hot blast of negative thoughts while about to hit the auto-dial before I noticed the disk on my passenger seat. And froze. You'd have thought it was a bomb about to go off and I was locked into the last millisecond before oblivion the way I stared at the thing, because it made no sense to me. I mean, like, it wasn't there when I parked my car, y'know.

Keeping the phone ready, just in case, I carefully picked the disk up and looked at it more closely, as if that would make it appear to be something else, something that did make sense. But no, it was what it was – a thin silver pancake of Lucite or something, shined to perfection and protected by a slipcase, with a cellophane window showing that nothing was written on it. I did notice it was actually a writable DVD instead of a CD...but that only added to my confusion.

You know, at that moment I really think I gained a vague awareness of how Alzheimer's sufferers must feel when they see something and they know they should know what it is but just plain cannot figure out the why or where or how of it. At the same time, I knew in a flash that Ms. Calvert had left it, once she knew for certain I was working in the restaurant. But then why would she even need to come in the restaurant? My car and its license plate number were in Grant's police report, so she'd have no trouble finding it on the street. Besides, how many white 1965 Volvo 122-S four doors were there in LA? But I also knew she knew I'd taken that copy of the video Allen had made, so I had no need for a DVD of it. Hell, I'd destroyed that friggin' thing, it so disgusted me. So was this meant to rub my nose in what her bastard boss and half the world thought of me? Was this the final twist of the knife? Did they know just how emotionally fragile I was, and were they now deliberately trying to "Gaslight" me into taking that final step to nothingness to spare asshole Allen any further embarrassment?

No. No, if I knew anything from that meeting, I knew Ms. Calvert was not happy about what Lewis was pulling. I could read it, even then, even in the midst of turmoil – in her actions, in her hurt expressions, in her deliberate and forced silence. So there was some other reason for this. But...what?

Well...there was only one way to find out. "Crash and burn" would have to wait for a while; this little detour seemed too important not to follow. I closed my cell phone, started my car and drove home, all on auto-pilot. I didn't think about the disk the entire way. I couldn't. No matter what scenario I came up with, I knew I'd find the truth would be completely different. So I left it alone until I was back in my apartment and had my TV on and the disk popped into my cheap-assed DVD Player and Jag freshly walked and fed and seated on the couch beside me, offering support in exchange for a scratch behind the ears (the slut of a mutt).

The disk loaded up a black screen, no menu. I was about to hit "play" when a logo swirled into view. "A LAWless West Presentation." What, this was a criminal law symposium? A learning tape for legal nitwits of the 19th Century? An ongoing discussion on the merits of Harley motorbikes over Bugattis? I almost laughed at that one. Then came the title – "The Snotty Waiter Who Asked For It." Starring Dick Long (oh, subtle, and appallingly dumb) and Jack Himov (even dumber). And then an image followed.

It was me. Walking down Melrose. Pissed as hell. As some guy said in a wooden voice-over, "There he is. That's the waiter that pissed me off. He served my steak cold."

"Okay then, let's teach him a lesson," drifted from the speakers. In Allen's voice. They stated to follow me in the van (that was new; the version I wound up with must have been an early edit). The next shot had me lying in the back of the van, bound and gagged and blindfolded and fully dressed, with Allen saying, "I'll show you how to serve meat right."

I hit "stop." And it wasn't because I couldn't watch this crap, again. Nor was it due to the fact that the dialogue was really REALLY bad. It was because I now understood why Ms. Calvert had dropped by, that evening – she was on my side. She didn't like what happened any more than I did and wanted me to know. And she was using this silly roundabout way of delivery so I couldn't really link it back to her – not in a court of law, anyway. And so she could also fill me in on a little secret – that Allen had been selling the video he did of me.

The mother-fucking son-of-a-bitch. No wonder he had me sign a release.

It's funny, but the realization didn't make all that much of an impression. No anger. No revulsion. I honestly do not think I was even surprised. In fact, my mental comment about Allen and his momma was expressed matter-of-factly, not with venom. It was just one more layer in this mess of a situation. But it did get me to wondering.

I went to my old iMac (on its last legs, the poor thing) and logged on to the internet. It didn't take long to Google up a website for "LAWless West Productions." Turned out they're a clearinghouse for fetish movies of every sort. Fisting. Waterworks. Enemas. Various forms of disgusting scatological interplay. Leather. Feet. He-She self service. Daddies. Male. Female. Bi. The works. Which included bondage – gay or straight or both. Having already come this far and already suspecting what I'd find, I clicked on the link for "Bondage – Gay."

Up popped another menu of various themes. "Breakin' In." "Kidnap." "He Asked For It." "Hitchhiker." "Chains." "Teen Boys."

"Ropes." "Rip 'n Strip." "Gang Bang." "Forced Naked." Needless to say, I chose the link to "He Asked For It."

A selection of twelve videos & DVDs appeared, each with a variation of the heading worked into the title. I located "The Snotty Waiter Who Asked For It." Number nine in the list. My fingers shook as I opened it...and up popped a copy of the cover with four thumbnail images as a teaser – me tied up in the truck, me lying on the bed, Allen "servicing" me and me spread eagle face-down on the bed as he...as he prepared for the grand finale. To view a two minute segment of the video would cost $2.99, on-line check or credit card, please, or I could buy tokens through a third party vendor...or I could add the DVD to my cart and keep on shoppin'.

I shut the computer down, instead, slipped the disk back in its envelope, turned my DVD Player and lights off and crashed atop my bed still fully dressed. Jag jumped up beside me and settled in on my right. I idly scratched his ears as I stared at my flat white ceiling. My mind stayed completely blank.

I was no longer even the least little bit into my crash and burn. There was no self-loathing giggle behind my blankness. No self-indulgent hatred of my own cruelty and actions. No wailing about my lot in life. No certainty I was guilty of murder by proxy. No wondering if I could ever forgive myself. No blame placed on anyone else (meaning Allen and his bastard buddies). Everything had been put on hold. Perhaps indefinitely. I didn't know. I didn't care. I just lay there. I did not sleep. I did not think. I did not move except to slowly stroke Jag's back.

The night drifted past in its own time. Not long. Not short. Just real. The dark room was quiet. Still. At rest with me. Vague moonlight filtered in, reflecting hints of shadows on the ceiling. I slowly grew aware of how many shades of night there are. How many shifting colors of grey. Some whispery. Some warm. Some thin and cold. Some deep and mysterious. Some welcoming. All blending together in my crowded little life to add room where there once was none.

Even the silence was grey. Nothing harsh or sharp or startling shrieked at me, that night, not from the street or the sky or my neighbors' abodes. Nor was there an absence of sound. Just the eternal breath of gentle existence flowing in, flowing out. Soft in. Soft out.

I felt at peace. Complete and utter peace for the first time in... well, honestly, in my life. Not tired. Not sad. Not weary of the world. Not angry. I was just...pleased about lying there, if that can make sense. Pleased because it meant nothing. Not one thing more than what it was. And I savored it. I drifted in it. Floated upon it. Let it hold me and caress me and make love to me in its nothingness. Let it banish any disturbance against my quietude. Even Jag, who can sometimes be restless as he sleeps, lay as still as death.

Just as the day was beginning to make itself known to the night, again, I felt something whisper over the tips of my hair. And lay itself on the left side of my face. It was like someone's left hand covering me from the top of my eyebrow to the line of my chin, its little finger nestled in the crook of my eye by the bridge of my nose. It was cozy. Warm. Exquisite in its strength and tenderness. I felt as though I knew it would come. Hoped it would. So when it did, I rolled my face into it. Let it glide over my nose and caress my right eye and drift soft against my right cheek. Its thumb drew gentle across my lips. I felt as though I'd been kissed. The fingers trailed down my neck and whispered away. I don't know whose hand it was – Bobby's, God's, my guardian angel's, my imagination's – it didn't matter. I felt so light and easy, I smiled and went to sleep.

I woke seventeen hours later to Jag whining at the door. He'd already let out a couple of puddles in my skanky rug, but there was no way in hell he'd do something he knew would piss the boss off completely. Poor guy. I hadn't been the best companion to him.

I got up, peed and took him straight out for a long walk in the night air. All the way down to Santa Monica Beach, where we romped in the cold sand and dark surf under and around the pier, keeping an eye out for guards and cops (no dogs allowed, don't ya know). The pier was almost deserted, the vast majority of its gaudy lights and childlike rides shut off. There were still people around – fishermen and trinket vendors and restaurant workers heading home and last minute lovers and tourists out for a quiet stroll over the relatively new boards as a gentle "Coastal Eddy" drifted in. Jag and I studiously ignored them all.

We both got sopping wet and cold, but I didn't care. Didn't even notice, really. It was too perfect.

On the way home, I bought us both roast beef sandwiches at Norm's Diner (open 24/7), and we sat under a vapor lamp lighting the parking lot next to it. This is a more industrial area of Santa Monica, low flat brick and stucco sided buildings painted non-colors with a power relay station and car wash and Denny's and offices on the corners and steady traffic along Lincoln, even after midnight on a Wednesday. All so very common and simple and plain. But wrapped in the light fog, the area struck me as mysterious and magical. I looked around, enthralled, as I fed Jag his sandwich and I munched on mine. I even shared a cup of water with him; after all I'd been through, I wasn't worried about a few doggie germs.

We got home at close to two, but I still bathed Jag and rubbed him down and made him the happiest mutt in the whole wide world. He was asleep on the couch before I had my sheets changed. I then showered and shaved and flopped on the fresh clean linen, naked, and slept till nine.

The next morning, I washed everything I owned that could be washed and ironed my shirt and slacks. Then, since I wasn't due to work till six that evening, I sat down at my computer and calmly, coolly and oh-so-casually began my research into William Allen Barrow and his buddies – starting with LAWless West Productions.

ABOUT THE AUTHOR

Kyle Michel Sullivan is an award-winning writer whose sole purpose in life is to tell stories and make his characters more real than the people he actually knows. After all, only fictional humans can truly understand him and be willing to talk to him at any time he wishes. He also sketches and paints and dreams of making movies and living in Seattle instead of the hell hole he currently inhabits.

Kyle Michel Sullivan is also the author of *How to Rape a Straight Guy, Porno Manifesto, Rape in Holding Cell 6 - Volume I and Bobby Carapisi - Volume I.* Available at Amazon.com, TheNazcaPlainsCorp. com or your local bookstore.

HOW TO
RAPE
A STRAIGHT GUY

Sometimes revenge is reason enough...

...but can it ever be the answer?

Kyle Michel Sullivan

Sullivan

HOW TO RAPE A STRAIGHT GUY

A
Boner
Book

Sullivan

PORNO
Manifesto

a novel by
Kyle Michel Sullivan

Porno Manifesto

A
Boner
Book

RAPE
IN HOLDING CELL 6
(VOLUME 1)

He set out to investigate the death of a friend...

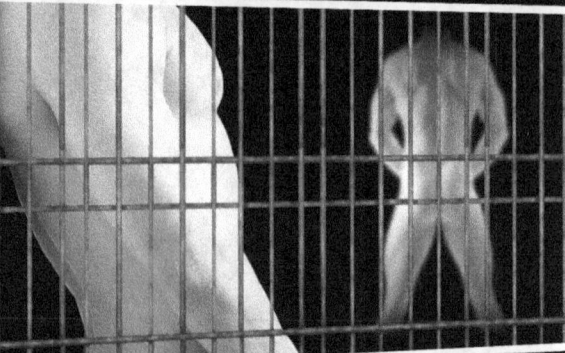

...but discovered a conspiracy of absolute evil.

A Novel of Erotic Suspense by
KYLE MICHEL SULLIVAN

A BONER BOOK

Sullivan

RAPE IN HOLDING CELL 6